THE FUT
ASSASSIN

by

G.D. Jones

Publish & Print
www.publishandprint.co.uk

ISBN: 9798647665430

Published by www.publishandprint.co.uk

Acknowledgements

Big thanks to Gilly Middleburgh for making this book as perfect as it could be with her world-class editorial skills, and for taking out all the 'Barbara Cartland' narrations and advising me to use my own voice.

Also, a huge thank you to my best friend Lori who unintentionally inspired me every day with her funny personality and hilarious quotes.

This book is dedicated to my parents Ann and Yank Jones, my brother-in-law Teeman Jason Worrall, and all the people who told me to stop dreaming and get a normal life.

CONTENTS

INTRODUCTION

Police community support officer and local hero, Jason Worrall's world is torn apart when his ex-wife and their five-year-old daughter are killed in an alleged car crash suicide.

One year on from that night's tragic events, with the Christmas holidays approaching, a reclusive Jason finds himself at the mercy of a strange young woman claiming to be none other than the mysterious hooded serial killer, known as the Future Assassin, who the police are desperately trying to find.

After she kidnaps him in a stolen taxi as she attempts to change future events and save the lives of innocent people, Jason is forced to accompany her from one destination to another, wherever the information written down inside a mysterious black book leads her.

PROLOGUE

It was close to midnight and Pembrey Forest was in almost complete darkness apart from the splashes of moonlight shining through the leafy branches of the trees, casting eerie shadows around a small clearing in which a lone hooded figure lingered before an ancient oak standing in solitary splendour as if it were the king of every other tree in the forest, its gnarled sagging branches curling to touch the ground and a huge hollow trunk sprouting a creepy humanoid face.

'I know you're here!' said the hooded figure in the angry voice of a woman. 'I haven't come all this way for nothing so you'd better come out from wherever you're hiding.' Throwing back the baggy hood of her cloak she revealed a young beautiful face with long black hair tied in a ponytail and green eyes that twinkled in the light of the moon. 'I'm not leaving until I speak to you so you'd better come out and face me. I don't care if I have to wait here all night,' she called, flashing her torch beam in every direction.

The forest remained still and quiet until the light from her torch began to flicker and she noticed her breath misting the air in front of her face as the temperature plummeted and the warm breezeless summer night took on a more wintery chill.

The surrounding trees, once so calm and peaceful, started to groan and creak as a sudden rush of wind pierced their branches, making them sway back and forth as if some unnatural force was sweeping its way through the forest charging the very air with a strange kind of energy that could never be described in words.

'What is it you want this time, child?' said a mysterious voice like a whisper being carried on the breeze.

'I need to speak to you about some information you gave me on my last visit here.' Her flickering torchlight pointed towards the tree as she pulled out a thick black book from one of the pockets in her cloak and tossed it to the ground near her feet. 'Something went wrong.'

'You were given lots of information on your last visit, child,' said the voice, sounding as if the wind itself was talking. 'Which part are you referring to?'

'Erm... let me think back...' said the woman in a voice filled with attitude. 'Does Saturday the ninth of August ring any bells? No? Well, allow me to refresh your memory. Fourteen-year-old Emily Evans raped and murdered while walking home from school in Cowbridge Road, Cumbria, by 55-year-old Patrick Baldwin from East Lancashire?'

'Yes, yes, child... I do remember. Did you not get there in time to save her?'

'Yes, she made it home safely,' replied the woman, rolling her eyes skywards.

'Then if the girl is safe and her attacker is dead why do you say something went wrong?' The eerie voice seemed a little more distant than before.

3

'Because I nearly ended up being killed myself in the process! The time, date and place you gave me were all accurate as usual. The man was parked up in a green Volvo along a narrow country lane, just like you said he'd be, waiting for the girl to pass by. But the one little detail you failed to fill me in on was that there was a second person sitting next to him in the passenger seat.'

'A second person?' said the voice.

'Yes... a woman. It could've been his wife or his girlfriend or even his sister, whatever... but the point is that you didn't mention anything about a woman being in the car as well. You let me find that one out for myself. And if I hadn't seen her in the corner of my eye coming at me with a knife I might have got my throat slit. How could you not have told me about her? I mean you're the one who sends me to these places. You're the one who should have all the facts straight before you have me jot them all down in that stupid book,' she said, kicking it into some tall grass. 'I'm just a woman on my own. You could at least be sure of what I'm dealing with before sending me on such a dangerous mission. If something happens to me who else is going to save all those people from their ill-fated futures?'

An extended silence followed, until the voice spoke again, closer this time. 'Not all the information given to you can be absolutely accurate. You knew this when you agreed to take on the task of saving these people from their would-be killers.'

'Yeah, I know that,' said the woman exhaustedly, 'but... '

'But nothing.' The voice cut her off. 'If you're looking for an excuse to back out now, then just leave… you can always be replaced.'

'Replaced?' laughed the woman. 'That's a good one. And just how are you going to find someone to replace me? I mean just take a look around this place. How many paranormal researchers and ghost hunters have deserted their tents and camping spots after getting a glimpse of you and your other equally ghoulish friends? Must be close to a thousand,' she chuckled. 'Let's face it, it took almost a decade for me to stop and listen to you, let alone believe that all this is actually possible. So I think we both know that no one is going to replace me any time soon.'

'Then why have you really come here, child?' the irritated voice interrupted, so close that she could almost feel it breathing down her neck.

'Rest assured, I didn't come here to quit,' said the woman not flinching. 'It's not a replacement I'm after, it's a partner.'

'A partner?' mocked the voice. 'Foolish girl, did you not just express how difficult it would be to convince another… so how do you expect to gain a partner?

'It would only be difficult for you to convince another. Me, on the other hand… well, let's just say I have better persuasion methods than someone like you. The fact of the matter is I can't do this alone any more. I need help and tonight you're going to help me find someone. And not just anyone… I want you to find someone tough and strong, someone who can cope with any situation… someone who I can trust to have my back at all times.'

'Such a silly naive little girl,' dismissed the voice. 'No one with such qualities would ever agree to assist you in what you are doing… unless… Yes, maybe there is someone who could help you…'

'Who? Tell me where to find this person,' said the woman in desperation, twigs breaking beneath her feet as she flashed her torch beam in all directions, still uncertain where the voice was coming from.

'Not so fast, child. The person I have in mind may be a gamble, and a risky one at that.'

'I don't care. You know I like a gamble,' replied the woman, her eyes sparkling with anticipation.

'Patience, child, patience. We must first step back and allow things to run their course before we do anything. We must give this person time.'

'Time for what?'

'Time to grieve… Time to regret… Time to have his heart consumed with rage and anger for all that the world has taken from him,' said the voice, increasing in volume with every word.

'Then what?' asked the woman, already guessing the answer.

'Then, child, that is when you will persuade him to join you.'

The woman flashed her torchlight back towards the ancient tree and smiled as a ghostly figure appeared from behind one of its sagging branches.

'Pick up your book, child. You must write this down... you must do exactly as I tell you...'

CHAPTER 1 - DESTINY WAITS

The honour of receiving an accolade for bravery at the annual Police Public Bravery awards ceremony in Manchester was just an illusion for any one person devoting their lives to serving their community. A desire one might say, or even a fantasy; nothing more than a silly pipe dream. But for police community support officer Jason Worrall that dream was now a reality.

At only thirty-four years of age this modest, hard-working and dedicated young man found himself the toast of the town with his picture on the front cover of every news magazine, looking every bit the hero with his handsome face and winning smile above the story of how he had single-handedly prevented three armed men from robbing a post office filled with innocent bystanders in his home town of Salford.

'A true hero,' was how the Lord Mayor of Manchester described him before presenting him with his gold medal, and even though it seemed fair to call him that, Jason hadn't intentionally tried to be one. He was just a regular person who had acted on impulse and hadn't given much thought to what he was doing until it was over. But with all the gratitude and admiration he had received from a community who were more than proud to know someone who had finally had the courage to stand up for what was right against the crime and violence that was slowly worsening on their streets, even he was starting to feel like some kind of super hero straight out of a comic book.

And after the praise and attention that most memorable day had brought, he now found himself standing on stage with a microphone in his hand in a room packed to the rafters with friends, family and work colleagues who had organised an after party for him in the town hall and were now gathering around in silence as their hero prepared to make a speech.

'Well, the first thing I should say is thank you,' said Jason, glancing away from the familiar and admiring faces in the crowd to take in the huge banner behind him with the words 'Thank you Jason' on it in big gold letters. 'Thanks to each and every one of you who made the effort to come tonight and to those who were responsible for putting together this wonderful celebration.' Jason smiled as a small round of applause began.

'You know,' he said, 'earlier today at the awards' ceremony I'd prepared a few words to say after I'd received my medal. As it turns out I wasn't permitted to say as much as a thank you but, on the bright side, at least I've been spared the embarrassment of having to make the same speech twice in one day!' Jason grinned and raked his fingers through his hair as the crowd laughed politely.

'But seriously,' he continued after clearing his throat. 'I feel very privileged to be standing in front of you all tonight because I know that there are probably a hundred or more people out there who are much more deserving of all this fuss than I am — and I'm not just talking about our fine community support officers, like the lovely lady I work with, my good friend Rachel Summers who, if I may say so, is looking very beautiful this evening.' Jason smiled while pointing to his colleague standing at the front of the crowd who was trying her best to hide her blushes.

'I'm talking about regular people,' said Jason, pausing momentarily to look at the faces in the crowd hanging on his every word. 'People who make a difference to other people's lives with a simple act or kind word when it's needed most; a person who is not afraid to give someone a chance when nobody else will; someone who would happily put their own problems aside to help another person in need. Those are the qualities that truly give a person the right to be called a hero...' Jason was suddenly lost for words as he spotted a young woman standing in the crowd holding a small girl in her arms.

'So, ladies and gentlemen,' said Jason finding his voice again after an extended silence. 'Before I leave this stage and re-join all of you to enjoy the rest of this wonderful celebration, I'd like to finish by saying that any one of us can make that difference – all we have to do is believe in ourselves and believe in each other.'

A deafening round of applause filled the hall as Jason finished his heartfelt speech and awkwardly placed the microphone back on its stand before rushing off the stage to catch up with the young woman and the child whom he could see moving away from the crowd, indicating that he should follow her to a quieter side of the room where they could talk in private.

Handshakes and countless hugs of gratitude greeted Jason as he made his way through the crowd doing his very best not to show his frustration at the many people unintentionally preventing him from joining the woman who was now waiting patiently for him near the entrance.

Fighting his way past his cheerful colleagues who had had way too much to drink, his over-excited family desperate to have him pose with them for just one memorable photo, and complete strangers who had clearly only shown up for the free buffet and complimentary glass of wine, Jason breathed a sigh of relief as he came face-to-face with Rachel.

'I'm so proud of you, Jase,' she said, greeting him with a warm hug.

'Thanks, Rach,' he said, seeming a little taken aback at how glamorous his friend was looking with her long blonde hair that he was so used to seeing in a ponytail, flowing over the jewelled cap sleeves of her blue dress. 'You look amazing!'

'That's two compliments I've had from you now,' said Rachel pretending to be shocked, 'and all in the space of five minutes.'

'What are you talking about?' said Jason, playing along. 'I'm always complimenting you.'

'You're such a liar,' laughed Rachel. 'You've never once complimented me in all the years that we've been friends.'

'Well, I am now,' said Jason with a mischievous grin, 'and I've got to say you scrub up really well.'

'Oh, cheeky!' She gave him a playful punch on the shoulder. 'You don't scrub up too badly yourself,' she giggled, while straightening the collar of his black suit jacket. 'Seriously, Jase, I may be wrong but I could swear I saw your ex-wife and your daughter standing among the crowd a few minutes ago.'

'You did,' said Jason, leaning closer to her so she could hear him above the noise in the room. 'They're both waiting for me over there, but as you've probably already guessed I'm finding it difficult to get to them.'

'Let me help you,' said Rachel, aware of her friend's frustration at his inability to cross the crowded room. Understanding the predicament he found himself in she linked her arm through his and began to lead him across the room, managing to avoid the well-wishers who continued their handshakes, congratulations and requests for photos, until they reached the other side where his ex-wife and daughter were standing.

The excited five-year-old left her mother's side and ran up to her father so she could shower him with hugs and kisses as he knelt down to greet her. 'Daddy, I missed you!' she said, cuddling him tightly as her barrage of kisses came to a sudden halt.

'I missed you too, sweetie,' he replied, picking up his little girl and greeting Jessica with a kiss on the cheek. 'I didn't think you'd make it.'

'We promised we'd be here, didn't we?' said Jessica with a smile. 'There's no way we were going to miss your big night, were we, Leona?' She chuckled as her little girl shook her head firmly and hugged her father once again.

'Well, if you'll excuse me I'll have to be getting back to my table,' said Rachel, feeling a little out of place as Jason and Jessica shared an affectionate look. 'If you need me for anything else just give me a shout.'

'Thanks, Rach,' said Jason as his friend smiled at them all and left. 'I can't tell you how happy I am now that you're both here.' He kissed his little girl, who looked almost identical to her mother with the same dark hair, blue eyes and pale skin, before putting her down but keeping hold of her hand. 'And what's even better is that you managed to come alone,' he said before noticing Jessica's nervous expression. 'Please tell me he didn't come with you?'

'Of course he did. How else were we supposed to get here?' replied Jessica. 'You know I don't drive and I couldn't exactly get a bus or a taxi all the way from Essex could I?'

'Couldn't you have caught a train?' Jason grumbled with a sour look on his face. 'And I'm guessing this means you still haven't told him about us?'

They were interrupted by a young man bringing Jessica a glass of white wine before she could even think about answering. 'Thanks, Harry,' she said, nervously sipping her Chardonnay with a look on her face that begged Jason to say no more on the subject.

'Harry, how nice of you to join us,' said Jason through gritted teeth. He tried hard not to lose his temper as the man he despised put his arm firmly around Jessica's shoulder telling Jason all he needed to know.

'Yeah, well it wasn't my idea to come here,' replied Harry noticing the unwelcoming look on Jason's face and the medal attached to his jacket. But your wife insisted. Oops! I meant to say your ex-wife.'

'Nice try, Harry,' answered Jason with a smile, 'but I refuse to have a battle of wits with an unarmed opponent.'

'Harry, would you take Leona to get some cake please?' said Jessica, interrupting the two men before their snide remarks turned into something more serious.

'Sure, why not?' said Harry as he and Jason stared each other out like two gunslingers from an old western.

'Leona, sweetie, I want you to go with your Uncle Harry. He's going to take you to get a slice of the huge chocolate cake we saw on the way in while Daddy and I have a little chat. Okay?' Jessica bent down to her little girl who seemed reluctant to leave her father's side until a stern look from her mother made her swap her daddy's hand for Harry's and she allowed herself to be led away.

'Catch you later, Uncle Harry,' Jason called out while grabbing a glass of champagne from a passing waitress. Harry turned to freeze him with a look before Leona tugged at his hand and pulled him through the crowds to get her share of cake while there was still some left.

'Jason, will you stop acting so bloody childishly,' said Jessica as Harry and Leona disappeared into the crowd. 'Can't you two pretend to like each other just for one night? You know how upset it makes Leona whenever you and Harry get involved in one of your slanging matches.'

'Well, he started it this time, not me. I was trying to be nice.'

'Oh, don't talk such rubbish,' spat Jessica. 'Anyone could tell by the look on your face that you can't stand the sight of him.'

'Is it really that obvious?' Jason slurped his glass of champagne.

'Yes, it is, and it's embarrassing to be quite honest,' said Jessica, banging her glass down on a small table, folding her arms and turning away from Jason in a huff.

'Well, what do you expect me to do? It makes my skin crawl to see that... that half-wit standing in my place next to you and Leona. Do you have any idea how hard it is for me to just stand there every time he's around and pretend that nothing is going on between us? I mean this is getting beyond a joke,

15

Jessica. When are you going to tell him that we're back together?'

'Jason, keep your voice down will you?' Jessica looked around nervously hoping that nobody was listening in on their conversation. 'Do you want the whole room to know our business?'

'Yes, I don't care who knows. You're my wife for crying out loud. I'm sick and tired of all this sneaking around.'

'Ex-wife, Jason, don't forget that. Now if you don't mind I think we should continue this conversation at a more convenient time when there aren't so many people around.'

'Fine, have it your way,' said Jason, downing the rest of his champagne and putting the empty glass down before grabbing Jessica by the wrist and escorting her through the entrance.

'Jason, what do you think you're doing?' Jessica protested as Jason led her round the corner of the building into a dark alley.

'Right,' said Jason letting go of her wrist. 'Now we're all alone so let's talk.'

'Jason, we can't stay out here, everyone will be wondering where you've got to.' Jessica folded her arms across her chest feeling the full effect of the chilly breeze through her lace dress.

'I'm sure they can manage without me for five minutes,' replied Jason, taking off his jacket and placing it around Jessica's shoulders to keep her warm. 'We have something that needs sorting out and I'm not moving from this spot until it's done.'

'Jason, I've told you over and over again, you have to stop pressuring me. You want things to happen right away, but it isn't that easy. You're just gonna have to be patient.'

'I've been patient,' said Jason, trying to hide his frustration with a half smile. 'I've waited and waited for you to tell him about us for eight months now and yet, here we are, still having to sneak around and hide down dark alleyways because you just don't have the heart to tell him we're back together.'

'Don't you think I've tried?' replied Jessica, her pencilled-on eyebrows raised and her voice high pitched. 'If only you knew just how many times I've come this close to telling him about us only to chicken out at the last second.'

'Look, I understand how difficult things must be for you, really I do, but can't you see that the longer you keep him in the dark the more it's gonna hurt when he does find out.'

'I know that,' said Jessica, her eyes closing in anguish. 'How did we get ourselves into such a mess?'

'It happens, Jess,' said Jason softly. 'People get married, they have their differences, sometimes they split up and go their separate ways until one day they realise that they made a huge mistake. We're not the first couple this has happened to and we won't be the last. Surely even someone as small-minded as Harry can understand that, if nothing else, at least for Leona's sake.'

'No! That's just it,' said Jessica in despair. 'That's the whole reason why things are so difficult. Harry loves Leona. He treats her as if she were his own. Losing her as well as me would destroy him, I know it.'

'But he's not her father, I am,' said Jason, running his fingers through his hair in despair. 'You and Leona are my family. He's just going to have to accept it, and if you haven't got the heart to tell him then may be it's time I did.'

'No, Jason,' said Jessica in panic, clutching at his arm to prevent him from going back inside and revealing all. 'Just hold on a minute. If anyone is going to tell him it's going to be me.'

'When though, Jessica, when?' he demanded.

'When the time is right...' Jessica responded with a shrug of her shoulders.

'But there's never going to be a right time. When are you going to realise that?' Jason was becoming more and more frustrated. 'Give me one good reason why we can't just walk back inside right now and tell Harry everything he needs to know?'

'Jason, are you serious?' asked Jessica in astonishment. 'Are you really willing to walk back into that room and break someone's heart in front of two hundred people? After all, you just said in your speech about people caring for one another... is that what you really want them to see?'

'Not really,' said Jason with a sigh realising how right Jessica was and that, as usual, he was letting his temper get the better of him.

'Well then, let me do this my way,' she said, stroking Jason's cheek in the hope of calming him down. 'Look, I know this is hard for you because it's hard for me too, but I promise that soon things will be just the way we planned with me, you and Leona being a proper family, but I need more time, surely you can grant me that?'

The sound of music and laughter from the hall spilled out onto the street as, much to Jessica's relief, Jason nodded his head in agreement. The noise reminded them both that time was getting on and soon they would have to emerge from their hiding place before suspicions were aroused.

'Come on,' said Jessica. 'Let's get you back inside before everyone starts to wonder what's become of their hero.'

'Oh, let them wonder,' replied Jason, as they shared a lengthy kiss under the starry night sky unaware of a suspicious Harry who had followed them outside and was lurking in the shadows listening in disbelief to every word.

*

The party was now in full swing, so much so that it seemed no one had noticed that Jason had been missing for the best part of twenty minutes as he and Jessica returned to the hall and headed back to the spot where she had left her drink. Beaming all over their faces and acting more like two love-struck teenagers than a divorced couple, they only remembered to unlink their arms when the sight of Harry standing by himself, head down staring at the floor, caught their attention.

'Harry,' said Jessica in concern, 'where is Leona?'

Harry ignored the question but continued to inspect the floor as if oblivious of Jason and Jessica standing next to him.

'Harry, where is Leona?' repeated Jessica, catching Jason's eye who looked equally concerned about the whereabouts of his daughter.

Coming out of his frozen state and turning his attention to Jessica Harry finally managed a reply. 'I left her with her grandparents,' he murmured. 'They insisted on taking her to get some cake.'

'Oh, right,' said Jessica seeming relieved until she noticed the look of anguish on Harry's face.

For him now it all made sense – the secret phone calls, the constant text messages Jessica had been receiving over the past year which, when questioned, she'd always brushed off as her sister calling or a friend messaging her on Facebook – had been Jason all along. He'd suspected as much but had been denying it to save himself from the kind of pain he now felt as he whispered, 'Where have you been?'

'We were just talking outside,' said Jessica guiltily. 'We couldn't hear ourselves think with all this noise,' she added, as she surreptitiously dug her heel into Jason's shoe to make him go along with her story.

Harry could hardly contain his anger as Jessica continued to explain herself with one feeble excuse after another, her voice becoming fainter and fainter as he fixed his gaze on Jason and swore to himself that there was no way on earth that he was going to let this man he despised take the only woman he had ever loved away from him, no matter what he had to do to make sure of it.

'Listen, do you mind if we leave a bit early?' he said, cutting Jessica off and leaving her somewhat confused.

'You want to leave now?' asked Jason, crushed by the very thought. 'But you've only just got here.'

'My boss has just called. Something very important has come up and he needs me to be at the office first thing in the morning,' Harry said to Jessica, completely ignoring Jason.

'You're needed at the office?' Jessica breathed a sigh of relief hoping that Harry's strange behaviour was down to work related issues and not because he was suspicious of her and Jason.

'I tried to explain the circumstances but you know how uncooperative he can be.' Harry loosened his tie, seeming more and more agitated with every passing second.

'Jason, I'm sorry but would you mind if we left a little early?' asked Jessica with regret in her voice.

'Well, yeah, I do mind,' said Jason, annoyed at the least that he was being asked such a question. 'But I don't suppose I have any say in the matter.

'Give us five minutes for Jason to say goodbye to Leona,' said Jessica, turning her attention back to Harry.

'I'll be waiting for you in the car,' Harry pushed his way past Jason and headed for the door.

'Oh, Jess, do you really have to leave so early? Can't you tell Harry you want to stay a bit longer? You and Leona could stay over at my place tonight if you want to. Then I'll take you both back to London first thing in the morning.'

'Jason, are you kidding?' Jessica suddenly remembered that his jacket was still around her shoulders. She shrugged it off quickly and handed it back to him. 'We almost got caught back there. If I ask him if I can stay until tomorrow he'll suspect something for certain. Please don's spoil our plans now.'

Jessica's wholehearted plea left Jason no choice but to agree as the two linked arms again and went to find their daughter.

*

The celebrations continued without incident as Jason said his goodbyes to Jessica and Leona after seeing them to the car. Harry waited impatiently with the engine running and both hands on the steering wheel, his gaze fixed firmly on the road ahead. He didn't turn his head as his passengers climbed in making themselves comfortable in their seats before waving Jason a final goodbye through the windows.

Gears crunched and wheels began to spin and before long Jason was left standing in a cloud of exhaust fumes unable to do anything but continue to wave until the car turned the corner and disappeared from view. It hurt him more than words could say to watch them go as it always did, each goodbye never failing to be harder than the last and always leaving a hole in his heart that could not be filled until he saw them again.

But now was not a time for being sad. He had a party to join and as hard as it might be for him to smile and be cheerful for those who thought so highly of him, he really had no choice. He wiped the tears from his eyes with his shirt sleeve and headed back into the hall wishing that the rest of the night's celebration would be over soon and take with it the impossible reputation that he had never wished for and would never be able to live up to.

More than anything he now wanted a second chance to be a proper father to the little girl he loved so dearly and a good husband to the woman who had always come second to his career. At long last the dream he had been craving seemed within his grasp – if only fate would be kind.

CHAPTER 2 - AFTER THE EVER AFTER

Was it early morning or late afternoon? Jason had no idea as loud knocking on his front door woke him from a deep sleep following yet another night of heavy drinking, leading as usual to him passing out on the sofa.

The young man who had once inspired a nation with his heroic act of bravery had long since departed and in his place left a heartbroken shell of a man, a recluse who spent most of his time alone in his house, hiding from the world using alcohol and anti-depressants to try and bury the grief of losing his ex-wife and his daughter a year before.

The police report detailing the crash which saw Harry's car collide head on with a cargo lorry on a busy main road in Salford confirmed that there were no suspicious circumstances surrounding the tragedy which took the lives of everyone involved.

Despite all the hard evidence that Jason had gathered to support his suspicions that the crash was caused by a suicidal act on Harry's part, nobody it seemed was ever going to believe that there was a lot more to the tragedy than the freak accident the police said it was. And why would they? It made no sense at all that a well respected young man like Harry, who was described by family and friends as a kind and generous soul with no history of violence whatsoever, could suddenly decide to do something so terrible and selfish as to take his own life and the lives of the two people he cared for so much. Even if he had discovered that something had been going on between Jessica and Jason it was unlikely that such a good-natured person would have done something so drastic to prevent it going any further.

Of course none of those loyal friends and family members had been witness to Harry's unusual behaviour the evening of the party just hours before the fatal crash; nor had they seen that unmistakable look of heartbreak in his eyes that could easily drive even the most civilised person into doing such an unthinkable thing. But Jason had and for him there was no doubt that somehow that night Harry had overheard his conversation with Jessica and in his anger, frustration and despair had used the most extreme measures to prevent them from ever being together. Harry and Harry alone was the one responsible for this devastating tragedy that had torn Jason's world apart and, no matter what any police report ruled out, nothing was ever going to convince him otherwise.

The loud knocking on the front door continued, followed by the door bell being pressed repeatedly, demanding Jason's attention. Still half asleep he sat up, putting his face in his hands to try and soothe the pounding headache that was surely going to be with him for the rest of the day, until he finally found the strength to get off the sofa and find out who was making such a commotion on the other side of the door.

After taking a quick look through the peep hole, Jason released the latch and opened the door to the tall young woman standing on the doorstep wearing a winter coat and carrying a small shopping bag.

'Hello, Rach.' Jason shaded his eyes from the bright morning sun and stepped aside to allow her to enter.

'Morning, Jase,' said Rachel clearing the snow off her shoes and wasting little time in getting out of the cold. 'Just paying my weekly visit.'

Jason closed the door and tried to snap himself out of his drowsy state. 'I wasn't expecting you until tomorrow,' he said, somewhat embarrassed that he had been caught off-guard, half awake and dressed only in a T-shirt and shorts.

'Yeah, I know, but I have such a busy week ahead, with it being the Christmas holidays and all. Today is the only chance I have to spend some time with you,' Rachel apologised before making her way into the living room with Jason following slowly behind her. 'I've been to the shop and bought some groceries and a few bits and bobs I thought you might need as well as today's Sun. If you wake yourself up a bit you can have a read while I make breakfast...' Rachel's voice trailed off after seeing what an awful state the room was in; empty bottles of booze spread over the floor and unfinished take-aways decomposing in their containers carelessly abandoned on any convenient surface.

Being the good-natured woman that she was and not wanting to give her friend a hard time for letting his home get into such a state, she pretended not to notice, acting as though everything was normal. She put her shopping bag on the sofa that had become Jason's bed for the past few months and went to the window to throw back the shutters so that the sun could spread some much needed light into the gloomy room.

'That's better,' she said, turning her attention back to Jason who had sunk onto the sofa again with his face in his hands. 'We'll give this place a good tidy up after we finish breakfast.' She took a look around, seeing the room in all its filthy splendour, before taking off her coat and scarf and carrying them into the kitchen with the bag of groceries.

'Rach, haven't I told you over and over that you don't have to come here every week to check up on me,' moaned Jason, leaning back against a cushion and trying to massage away his thumping headache.

'Oh, come on now. Paying you a visit once or twice a week is hardly checking up on you, is it? Rachel called out as she began to empty the groceries onto the kitchen table.

'Well, it certainly feels that way to me,' said Jason, wanting nothing more than to reclaim his sleep.

'OK, so maybe I am checking up on you,' Rachel confessed while making a racket searching inside every cupboard for a frying pan. 'But you're my best friend for crying out loud and it's not like you wouldn't do the same for me.'

'I know that,' said Jason, 'and I know you mean well but you've called at a really bad time and I just haven't got the energy for all this fuss so early in the morning.'

'Sorry, what was that?' Rachel, rattling her way through pots, pans and dishes in her search for the missing frying pan, couldn't hear Jason's low tones clearly. 'Jase, where have you put the frying pan? I hope you haven't tried hiding it.'

'I don't know where it is, and if I did I wouldn't tell you because I'm not hungry.'

'Now look here,' said Rachel storming out of the kitchen to confront Jason. 'We go through this every time I come here and you always end up getting your own way. But not today, mister, because I'm going to make you a delicious breakfast and you're going to eat it, is that clear?' She stood with her arms folded and eyebrows raised, speaking firmly as if to a small child.

'Shouldn't you be making breakfast for your husband and kids?' said Jason with a yawn.

'Gary is at work and the boys have gone Christmas shopping with their grandparents.'

'Shouldn't you be at work as well?' Jason was beginning to realise that Rachel was not giving up this time until he'd complied with her demands.

'My shift doesn't start until twelve. Now, frying pan, where have you hidden it?' she asked with a knowing smile.

'Try on top of the freezer.' Jason finally gave in with a heavy sigh.

'Now that's more like it.' Rachel headed back to the kitchen to investigate with Jason tagging along behind, dragging his feet on the carpet, after realising it was not going to do his thumping head any good to yell at her from opposite rooms.

'So how is the family keeping anyway?' said Jason with another yawn, taking a seat at the small breakfast table while Rachel retrieved the frying pan from its hiding place and put it on the stove.

'They're all fine, thanks,' said Rachel adding some oil to the pan. 'Gary's been flat out at work as usual and the boys are enjoying their time off school as you can imagine. I'm trying to persuade them to take part in the children's choir for the Christmas Eve mass but they don't seem too keen on the idea.' She laughed as she glanced at Jason and saw him with his face in his hands once again, nursing his hangover.

Sympathy got the better of her. 'Aw, Jason,' she said, if we don't do something about that head of yours you're not going to be able to enjoy your breakfast. Shall I pop back to the shop to get you some Alka Seltzer?'

'There's some on the top shelf,' replied Jason, freeing his hands and managing to push himself into a more upright position. 'But they won't work. Nothing works when it's this bad.'

'Well at least let's try,' said Rachel, standing on tiptoe and reaching for the packet awkwardly placed behind a variety of things that really didn't belong on a kitchen shelf.

At the same time, Jason took a sudden interest in the paper that Rachel had left on the table for him. FUTURE ASSASSIN KILLS AGAIN! read the headline on the front page with a story below it.

'Things are still as bad as ever on the streets I see,' he said, folding up the paper and chucking it back on the table while Rachel placed a glass of water in front of him with two tablets dissolving at the bottom.

'Same as ever I guess,' she said taking the chair next to him. 'You know how it is, quiet one minute, chaos the next. Don't suppose you heard that Rick Daxton, one of the three guys you prevented from robbing that post office, has an appeal coming up in a few weeks time. It's doubtful he'll get the early release he's hoping for though.'

She picked up the paper from the table, showing Jason a story further down the page. 'Have you seen this? Everybody's talking about it. It's on all the front pages this morning and all over breakfast TV.'

"A 57-year-old woman has given a statement following a police appeal for anyone to come forward with information on the death of a 32-year-old man whose body was found beside a canal near the Norfolk Broads in the early hours of Friday morning with gunshot wounds to his chest and leg," she read aloud. "The woman, who has not been named, is believed to have told police in her statement that around 5.15 on Thursday afternoon while walking her dog, she was approached from behind by a man with a knife, later identified as James Owens of no fixed abode. As he attempted to snatch her bag a hooded figure appeared out of nowhere and shot Owens several times before disappearing into the night..."

Jason rolled his eyes and couldn't have looked less interested if he'd tried as Rachel continued to read the rest of the story quietly to herself. 'Rach, you're welcome to take that paper home with you and spend the rest of the morning reading all of the rubbish in it if it means that I can go back to sleep,' he moaned before taking a deep breath and downing his glass of water even though the tablets inside hadn't had enough time to dissolve completely.

'Come on now, it can't all be rubbish.' Rachel lowered the paper and looked at Jason who was pulling a disgusted face from the awful taste of the medicine. 'Over twenty assassinations in the past year alone, with dozens of eye witnesses all telling the same story of a hooded figure appearing out of nowhere to save them from danger. I don't know if the person responsible for these murders is from the future like the papers are saying, but you have to admit it's all pretty weird... and frightening too.'

She folded the paper neatly and put it back on the table before returning to the stove. 'I can tell you're not very interested,' she said, busily filling the pan with rashers of bacon, 'but there are dozens of other stories in there. It might do you some good to know what's going on in the world.'

'I'm not interested in what's happening in the world,' said Jason coldly. 'The world is a cruel place. I don't need a cheap newspaper to remind me of that.'

'You didn't always feel that way,' said Rachel, disposing of the empty bacon packet in the rubbish. 'I remember a time not so long ago when you had nothing but optimism for this world we live in.' She smiled to herself before having to block her nose from the awful smell of garbage as she stuck her hand into the bin to retrieve something that had caught her attention almost buried beneath all the empty take-away cartons, pizza boxes and beer cans inside.

'Jase, what is this doing in the rubbish?' Rachel asked, carefully lifting out a badly damaged photo frame containing a picture of Jason standing proudly by the Lord Mayor having been presented with his gold medal at the Police Bravery Awards ceremony in Manchester. Both the picture and the medal placed next to it were now barely visible through the shattered glass.

'Because that's where it belongs!' spat Jason, unable even to take a look as Rachel undid the clips at the back of the silver frame so that she could get to the photo and the medal attached to the mounting board inside.

'You're lucky it's only the frame and the glass that are damaged,' said Rachel, dropping the broken frame in the rubbish and sitting next to Jason again, placing the mounting board on the table in front of her. 'This has been up on your wall for less than a month and already you've trashed it.

Destroying your TV and mobile phone were bad enough but at least those can be replaced. Not many people are privileged enough to have something like this hanging in their living room awarded for inspiring the nation.' She carefully inspected both the picture and the medal for any unseen damage.

'Some inspiration I turned out to be, causing the death of my wife and child,' said Jason, his bottom lip beginning to quiver and his eyes filling up with tears.

'Jason, you mustn't talk like that, it isn't true.'

'It is true, Rach.' The tears were starting to roll down his face. 'If I had just left them alone… if I hadn't come between her and Harry, none of this would've happened.'

'But none of this is your fault. It was just an accident, just a terrible accident, nothing more.' Rachel moved her chair closer to Jason's and grasped his hand.

'It was no accident, Rach. He knew about me and Jess. I saw the look on his face that night… he knew.'

'You'll never know that for sure. Look, I know you're angry and I know you're trying to make some kind of sense out of all this, but you can't carry on this way, Jason, you have to get on with your life. Jessica and Leona would have hated seeing you like this, drinking yourself into oblivion day and night and never leaving the house. This has to stop, Jason. You've got to move on.'

'How can I move on, Rach?... I've got nothing left,' said Jason, drying his eyes on the sleeve of his T-shirt.

'Yes you have,' she said, her dark eyes full of concern. 'You've got me and dozens of other friends who really care about you whether you realise it or not. And then there are your parents; your poor mother is worried sick about you. You never answer the door to her when she comes here or pick up the phone when she rings. All she wants is to know is how you're coping and it's sad that she has to find out from me, seeing that I'm the only person you'll speak to. Look, I know it's easy to say this to you from where I'm sitting but all I'm trying to say is that you don't have to do this alone. You have people who are here for you, so maybe it's time you stopped shutting everyone out and hiding away from the world. You know you're always welcome at my place and I'm sure that your parents would be over the moon if you paid them a visit.'

'I appreciate you trying to help me, Rach,' said Jason, managing a smile, 'but if it's all the same to you I'd rather not. You have your own family to look after and don't need me as an extra burden. And I can't go to my parent's house because if I do they'll beg me to stay and we'll just end up having an argument. I really don't need all that right now. Besides my mother has enough to worry about with looking after Dad so it's better for everyone if I just keep away.'

'You wouldn't be a burden, Jase, so don't say things like that. And if you explain to your parents, quietly and calmly before you pay them a visit, that you don't want to stay, I'm almost certain they'd understand.'

'No, I don't want to,' he said. 'I just want to be left alone. Apart from seeing you and making a trip to the off-licence once or twice a week I'm not interested in seeing or speaking to anyone or leaving this house ever again.'

Rachel breathed a sigh of defeat as it finally began to dawn on her that nothing she could say or do, despite her best efforts, was ever going to bring Jason out of his unhappy and reclusive state. The truth was, though until that morning she had refused to admit it to herself, that Jason's condition was not improving. His reckless drinking was out of control and with each visit he seemed to be a little paler and more fragile than before.

She was losing him; piece by piece she was losing her best friend and there was nothing she could do to help him. Feelings of guilt, worthlessness, and long spells of depression were all part of the grieving process. She knew that from experience having lost her mother to lung cancer when she was just fourteen. But this was different. This was not simply a person grieving over the loss of a loved one, but a person who had completely lost the will to live.

And if things carried on as they were, if she could not find a way to help Jason soon, the dreaded day would no doubt arrive when her phone calls to him would go unanswered and her knocks on his front door would be greeted with silence.

Time was running out and it was becoming clear that Jason was close to reaching the point of no return.

But despite knowing all of this, despite the fact that Jason appeared to be on a downward spiral, despite all the signs she had chosen to ignore over the past weeks which indicated that she was fighting a losing battle; despite all these things and more which had kept her awake at night with worry, Rachel had to cling on to the small shred of hope that somewhere, deep inside, buried under the pain and heartache, the old Jason, the kind and courageous soul she had known since they were both children, was still in there somewhere trying desperately to find a way out of the dark and desolate place where he was imprisoned. And for that reason alone she could not give up on him, she would not give up hope no matter how little there was left to cling on to.

A spitting, crackling sound suddenly brought Rachel out of her reverie reminding her to check on the bacon rashers she had left sizzling in the frying pan before they became inedible.

Having turned off the flame she returned to her seat next to Jason. 'OK let's put things into perspective shall we? If you carry on like this... living the way you are now, if you don't make some sort of effort to get yourself out of the house and start existing in the real world again, this time next year, Jase, you might be... well, quite frankly you might not be here anymore,' said Rachel, trying not to sound too harsh with her brutal honesty.

'I don't care. I don't know how it would matter to anyone anyway,' replied Jason, not seeming the least bit concerned for his own wellbeing.

'It matters to me.' Rachel thumped her fist on the table. 'Don't you even care how I would feel if something bad were to happen to you?' Doesn't it bother you that I might come here one morning and find you lying lifeless on the floor?' she said in despair.

'Of course it bothers me.'

'Well then, can't you at least try to turn things around now while you still can, for my sake?'

'I really wish I could, Rach, but it's not that easy.' Jason closed his eyes and let out a deep sigh.

'I'm not saying it's going to be easy but the more you push yourself the easier it will become, I promise,' she said, determined to be heard. 'Go and visit your parents on Christmas Day, or come over to mine for Christmas dinner, whatever you decide to do it has to be better than staying in here all day by yourself. Even if you only attend mass on Christmas morning at least you'll be getting out of the house for an hour or so.'

'Say, that's an idea,' said Rachel, acting as if she had just had a brainwave. 'Why didn't I think of that before?' She smiled as Jason looked at her curiously. 'You could come with me to the Christmas Eve mass at the Cathedral. That would be a perfect way for you to get out of the house for the evening and you'd be somewhere you could sit quietly without having to worry about anyone bothering you. You'd be helping me out because if I tell the boys that you're coming to see them sing they'll have no choice but to take part in the children's choir. And not only that, but your parents will most likely be there too so it will give them a chance to spend some time with you. We could even share the same pew if I arrange it. Oh, please say you'll come, Jason, please.'

He ran his fingers through his hair and tried to think of a kind way of telling her without being offensive that he wasn't in the least bit interested in her proposal. 'I don't know, Rach. It's been so long since I went to church. I don't know if I could face it after everything that's happened this year. It might end up doing more harm than good.'

'It won't. You'll be fine. Besides I'll be right next to you and if it all gets too much you can leave at any time, so please say you'll come... for me?' She pulled a pretend sad face.

Jason seemed lost for words. The very thought of spending any time in the company of a whole congregation, composed mostly of gossip mongers and busybodies who loved nothing better than to relish someone else's troubles, was enough to make him want to lock his front door and never again leave the privacy of his own home. But after everything that Rachel had done for him, how could he even think about refusing to do this one thing in return for all her help and support and sheer determination not to walk away and give up on him even when he had given her good reason to do so?

After taking all of this into consideration and realising that Rachel, as always, had his best interests at heart, he knew that there was really only one thing he could say, however reluctantly.

'OK, I'll come,' he said.

'Oh, thank you, Jase, thank you,' she said with delight, springing up from her chair to give him a massive hug.

'Ouch, watch the head, please watch the head,' moaned Jason, his headache returning with a vengeance as she stepped back to allow him some breathing space.

'Sorry,' she giggled, half embarrassed. 'I got a bit carried away. I'm just so excited.'

'Well, don't get too carried away because I'm only going to the mass. Straight there and straight back so don't get any other ideas,' he warned.

'I won't, I promise.' Rachel moved the mounting board from the table to a place of safety on the worktop and went to the sink to wash her hands. 'Now, in the meantime, I'll get these bacon butties ready and then later I'll see if I can get this reframed for you.' She looked fondly at Jason's picture wondering if the man she saw there could ever return or whether he was gone forever.

After finishing breakfast and giving the house a much needed tidy up, Jason showed Rachel to the door, seeming a little brighter and far less moody than he had only an hour or so before.

'Thanks for making breakfast and for... err... cleaning the place up,' said Jason.

'Don't mention it.' She stepped out into the cold but turned back. 'Just make sure you get some rest until that headache of yours cools off and, please, whatever you do, try not to have any more alcohol.'

'I'll do my best,' Jason yawned.

'Good,' smiled Rachel, acting as if she believed him if only for a second. 'Now if you need anything else before I come again don't be afraid to call me, OK?' She rummaged inside her handbag trying to find her car keys.

'Thanks, Rach.' He smiled gratefully as they shared a farewell hug.

Rachel glanced at her watch. 'Well, I'd best get a move on, my shift starts soon. Don't forget now, the Christmas Eve mass starts at six o'clock at the Cathedral.'

She headed down the snow-covered path to reach her car which was parked up on the kerb in front of the house. 'I'll ring you on the day just to remind you,' she called. Jason gave her a thumbs up as she unlocked her door and got in.

After exchanging goodbye waves the car slowly pulled away, melting snow and ice sliding off the roof and windows as it picked up speed and turned on to the next street, allowing Jason to close his door to the world and sink back into his usual lethargy.

CHAPTER 3 - A FACE FROM THE PAST

The sound of a voice screaming in terror accompanied by some overly dramatic music blared from the television bringing Jason suddenly out of his unconscious state, forcing him to rummage around for the TV remote on the sofa where he had nodded off while flicking through the channels.

His head still pounded from the previous night and his eyelids were heavy. An unsuccessful search finally led him to the only other place the remote could be hiding – on the floor next to his feet – having slipped through his fingers when he drifted off to sleep like so many times before. Having found the remote and replaced the batteries which had fallen out when it hit the floor, Jason wasted little time in switching off the black and white film adaptation of Dickens' *A Christmas Carol* just as the ghostly figure of a man covered in chains appeared on screen to confront the skinny old miser who sat quivering in his armchair.

'How long have I been out?' Jason wondered as silence descended and only a shard of moonlight coming through the crack in the curtains allowed him to see the clock on the wall which read 5.44 p.m. 'Is that all it is?' he sighed, leaning his head back on a cushion and rubbing his eyes. If it had only been a couple of hours closer to ten o'clock he might have headed straight to bed and probably wouldn't have given a second's thought to opening the small bottle of scotch he had hidden from Rachel behind the cabinet while she was busily tidying up. But it wasn't even six o'clock yet and Jason knew there was no way on earth he could get through the long and lonely hours without the aid of alcohol.

He staggered to the hallway and flicked on the light, then nearly tripped up on one of his socks as he dragged his feet over the carpet and headed back towards the cabinet next to the TV, moving some of the DVDs from his movie collection on the top shelf only to discover that his precious bottle of Famous Grouse was nowhere to be seen.

Had Rachel caught him in the act and pretended not to notice, he wondered, while going through each DVD on every shelf to make sure he hadn't made a mistake and that his eyes weren't playing tricks on him. No luck. 'But she couldn't have seen me,' Jason thought. 'It's impossible.' He had made sure she wasn't watching when he retrieved the bottle from under a cushion on the sofa and had waited until her back was turned before stashing it out of sight. He was almost certain that he hadn't left the room until she had finished cleaning, but then he remembered that she had asked him to fetch the vacuum cleaner from the cupboard under the stairs which would have given her more than enough time to find the bottle and dispose of its contents down the sink.

Jason's suspicions were soon realised after a quick investigation into a few of the rubbish bags placed at the side of the house led him to find the missing bottle with not a drop of scotch left inside. 'Aww, Rach,' he moaned, throwing the empty bottle back into the bag, frustrated that he was being treated like a child, but even more frustrated that there was no other choice but to get dressed and take the long trek down the road to the off-licence.

*

Jason entered the corner shop and the door alert chimed loudly as he threw back the hood of his coat, took off his gloves and shoved them inside his pocket. Hoping no one would recognise him in his black woolly hat he joined the short queue to the counter where an Asian gentleman with a long greyish beard was busy serving.

'Large bottle of Bannoch Brae please, Mr Shah,' said Jason, reaching into his wallet while looking at the variety of bottles on display behind the counter.

'I am very sorry, sir, but I cannot serve you,' said the shopkeeper narrowing his eyes.

'Excuse me?' said Jason, surprised and a little taken aback by what he was hearing.

'Your lady friend came in here earlier today and strongly advised me not to serve you any more alcohol due to the harm that you are supposedly doing to yourself,' said the shopkeeper, folding his arms and looking at Jason sternly.

'Lady friend?' Jason frowned in confusion before realising that Rachel was the lady he was referring to.

'Listen,' said Jason with a chuckle. 'Whatever she's said about me I can assure you it's all nonsense. She's just a worrier that's all and sometimes she over reacts. Now just give me what I've asked for and I'll be on my way.'

Still the shop keeper's expression remained stern. 'I'm very sorry, sir, but I still cannot serve you any alcohol. I must take your lady friend's advice.'

'Oh, for heaven's sake, this is ridiculous.' Jason huffed in frustration. 'You mean to tell me that I've been coming in here for over six months and now you're refusing to serve me because of a bit of hearsay?'

'Please, Mr Worrall, kindly lower your voice.' The shopkeeper leant closer in an effort to calm Jason down. 'Now I did not say I cannot serve you, I merely said that I cannot serve you any more alcohol. You're very welcome to buy anything else from the store.'

'I don't want anything else,' Jason shouted, slamming his fist on the counter before taking a deep breath and trying to control himself having noticed the long queue forming behind him. 'Listen, all I want is a bottle of scotch, even if it's only a small one, and then I promise I won't trouble you any longer. Please?'

I'm so very sorry, sir. I'm afraid the answer is still no,' said the shop keeper after a moment's hesitation.

'Fine! Don't serve me then,' Jason spat. 'I'll just have to get it from some place else won't I?' he yelled before purposely knocking a tray of loose sweets off the counter and pushing his way past shocked customers on his way to the door.

Outside he stopped to take in his surroundings, his breath misting the air in front of his face as he contemplated his next move. The nearest place he could buy alcohol was over two miles away in town. If it had been on any other occasion Jason wouldn't have even thought twice about taking the hour-long walk there and back, but the snow on the ground was already three inches thick and beginning to come down again even more heavily with no sign of it easing off. He was left with only two options; either he could take a taxi into town where there was a convenience store on almost every corner, or he could just go home, forget about the whole thing, and try to sleep it off until the morning.

But the thought of going home empty handed did not appeal to him in the slightest, nor did catching a cab into town and having to exchange unwanted conversation with a complete stranger. As he stood on the darkened street contemplating his next move, the lights from the Christmas decorations on the pub across the road caught his attention and a more-than-desperate Jason found himself tempted to do the unthinkable and cross the road to visit the shabby-looking red brick public house that from the outside looked neither warm nor welcoming.

A plan came to mind, which felt simple enough. All he had to do was walk inside, order a large bottle of alcohol with the highest volume, and make a quick exit before any heads turned; and if all went well he could be in and out of there in less than five minutes. Of course, going into a pub at that time of day would always bring the risk of bumping into someone he might know, but any course of action that he was forced to take now that his local shop had refused to serve him offered that same risk whether he liked it or not.

After taking all things into consideration Jason found himself crossing the slushy main road and heading past the tall pub sign, which read 'The Duchy Inn'.

*

The delightful aroma of roast dinner and cool ale assailed Jason's nose as he entered the lively pub and gazed around its crowded room. He almost changed his mind and would have made a sharp exit if not for the little voice in his head persuading him with every step that if he had been brave enough to come this far then surely he could make it to the bar to be served.

All around him people were standing, talking, laughing and having fun oblivious to the lone figure squeezing his way past them on his way to order a drink. Bright disco lights flashed in every corner of the shabbily decorated room and a female vocalist with an acoustic guitar crooned her way through a sad Christmas song while couples swayed to the spellbinding music.

It had been so long since Jason had been in such an environment that he'd almost forgotten quite how much he hated the noise and nonsense of such places and found himself wishing that he had taken the exit route while he still had the chance. Finally he arrived at the bar and his thoughts were concentrated more on being served than on his imminent departure.

Standing on his right a scruffy looking skinhead, his chubby arms covered in tattoos, leant against the bar cradling a pint of beer and singing along loudly to the lyrics of the song being played while glancing over his shoulder and giving the busy barmaid a cheeky wink at every opportunity. To his left a couple of women who had clearly had too much to drink balanced themselves up against a couple of bar stools and Jason found himself smiling at one of the women's attempt to get her purse out of her handbag which ended with her staggering backwards dropping the entire contents onto the floor.

But the smile soon vanished as both women knelt on the floor in an effort to retrieve their belongings allowing Jason to see the person standing beside the two drunken women who until that moment had gone unnoticed. It was his old friend Steve from the police, off duty and busy chatting to his three companions as they waited to be served.

Thankfully, the women had caused so much of a commotion that his friend had not seen him and Jason quickly turned his back before he was spotted and recognised, planning his escape while he was still unnoticed. As much as he needed the drink he craved there was no way that he could risk being caught by his former colleague who had tried to visit him at home on several occasions, only to be met with silence every time.

After seeing an opening Jason made a quick dash for the door, but any hope he had of escaping was foiled as a party of men and women dressed up as Santas, elves and reindeers came into the pub singing and laughing, blocking Jason's departure and unintentionally forcing him back to the bar where he was brought face-to-face with Steve.

'Jason? Jason, my friend, it is you,' said Steve astonished to see the man who had made himself invisible for the past year now standing in front of him and inside his local of all places. 'It's good to see you,' he said grinning with pleasure despite receiving an awkward handshake and a reluctant hug in return.

'Hello, Steve.' Jason seemed strangely resigned as if he knew this moment had been coming.

'So, how are things with you, mate?' said Steve, acting as if not a week had gone by since they had last spoken.

'I'm fine... I'm doing just fine.' Jason forced a smile while avoiding his friend's gaze and looking for an easy escape route.

'Well, that's good to hear. I've been worried about you... I mean we all have,' said Steve, putting a hand on Jason's shoulder and steering him towards the bar. 'I don't know how many times I've called at your house to see how you're doing but you never seem to be in. Have you moved since we last spoke?'

'No. I've... err... been away. I haven't had a chance to see anyone lately. I've been trying to keep myself busy with stuff... you know...' The desperate tone in Jason's voice and the uneasy way he was acting made it clear as day that he wanted nothing more than to leave the company of his friend.

'Oh, right...' Steve sensed the tension and began to figure out that all was not as fine and dandy with Jason as he was making out as he took in the hollow cheeked, bearded face and bloodshot eyes that were begging for sleep. 'Well, listen, where are you sitting? I'll bring some drinks over and we'll have a proper chat. The lads won't mind, I'm sure.' He rolled his eyes at the rest of his friends who were far too busy fighting for the barmaid's attention to notice anything else as she served them in turn.

'I'd love to but I'm afraid I can't,' replied Jason, backing up a few paces not really taking care of where he was going. 'Maybe some other time though?'

'Yeah... of course, mate,' agreed Steve confused by Jason's strange behaviour. 'Tell you what, I'll see if I can call over to your house before the New Year. Maybe we could have a few drinks or something?'

'Sounds good. I'll see you soon, Steve.' Jason turned round in a hurry after seeing that the entrance was now clear only to bump into the skinhead still leaning against the bar and knocking the pint glass out of his hand.

'Why don't you watch where you're going, you bloody fool!' said the man, angered not only by the fact that his Man United T-shirt was now drenched in larger, but also that he had not received as much as an apology from Jason who beat a hasty retreat leaving him and Steve looking confused.

Once outside Jason stopped and leant against the door wishing that he'd never entered the pub in the first place and made such a show of himself. A roar of laughter echoed through from the pub and even though he knew better he couldn't help but feel that the whole place was laughing at him.

In the distance the faint sound of carol singers performing 'Silent Night' in perfect harmony caught Jason's attention as he slowly left the Duchy Inn, stopping only once to look at the huge decorated Christmas tree inside the pub's beer garden with an illuminated shiny star at the very top. It all added to his misery as he tore off his hat and threw it at the yellow star in anger for all the wishes that had not come true in his life.

Pulling up the hood of his coat Jason began the long walk home without noticing the silhouetted figure of a woman seated behind the wheel of a white taxi cab parked across the road who had been watching his every move for the best part of the evening – waiting like a predator stalking its prey.

Waiting, just waiting for her chance to strike.

CHAPTER 4 - THE GREEN-EYED MONSTER

An icy December wind blew hard against Jason's face as he trudged home through the deep snow that stretched out in front of him like a gleaming white carpet. Huge flakes continued to fall lazily from the sky, sticking to his coat and collecting on the rooftops of the houses he passed, some covered with brightly lit decorations and some with twinkling Christmas trees shining through the slush-covered windows transforming the unattractive Duchy Road council estate into a magical wonderland.

Jason, who until that moment hadn't thought about what he was going to do for the rest of the evening without the aid of some alcohol to help him through another night of bad dreams, carried on walking through the snow that was getting deeper with every step he took. He wished that he had stayed at home and avoided all the embarrassing events that the evening had brought, when the sound of an approaching car caught his attention and the glow from its headlights cast his shadow on the snow-covered pavement ahead of him. At first he thought the car was travelling at walking speed because of the poor driving conditions but a quick glance over his shoulder showed him that the car was in fact a taxi which was indicating left and its passenger window was slowly opening as it pulled alongside the kerb in front of him and came to a stop.

'Need a lift?' called the sultry voice of a woman, stopping him in his tracks.

'No, thanks, I really don't have far to go,' said Jason, registering that the driver was a young woman in her late twenties or early thirties.

'Don't be silly, you're gonna freeze to death out there,' said the woman speaking louder over the cab's noisy engine. She leant across the passenger seat so that Jason could hear her more clearly. 'Where are you headed?'

'Linden Avenue.' With snow crunching beneath his feet Jason walked towards the car and bent down to look through the window only to see a beautiful tanned face staring back at him with slanted green eyes that twinkled as they met his gaze.

'That's nearly a mile from here,' she said with a knowing smile showing off a set of perfect white teeth. 'You'll never make it if it carries on coming down like this.' Brushing a stray strand of her dark hair away from her cheek she added, 'I'm going past Linden Avenue anyway so you might as well jump in.'

Jason smiled at the young woman's persistence before looking up and seeing no lessening of the falling snow.

'You'd better hurry and make up your mind before we both get snowed in,' joked the woman as he hesitated wondering what to do.

A taxi was not Jason's favourite form of transport but tonight was different. As far as he was concerned it couldn't get any worse and the lift home seemed a better option than the half-hour journey it would be on foot if he refused, so after a second's hesitation he opened the passenger door and climbed inside the cab.

'Thanks', he said throwing back his hood and fastening his seat belt while the woman carefully manoeuvred the car back onto the road.

'My pleasure,' smiled the woman catching Jason gazing at her short black skirt and red low-cut top. 'Are you crazy walking out in this? Hardly a night for a stroll, is it?' She closed the passenger window and turned the windscreen wipers on full. 'Needed to clear your head, I guess?'

'Yeah, you could say that.' Jason was unable to stop himself from taking sidelong glances at the strange young driver whom, he had to admit, was bringing back feelings that until then he believed no longer existed inside him.

Apart from Rachel Jason had not been in female company for quite some time, and even though he never imagined ever looking at another woman after losing Jessica, there was no denying that he found this woman attractive. As guilty as it made him feel, he was finding it hard to keep his eyes off her. Everything about her was so perfect, from her tight-fitting clothing that complimented her slim figure, to her long hair, tanned skin, almond-shaped eyes and sharp features that seemed to match the strangeness in her accent which sounded neither familiar nor unfamiliar. It was definitely British, but from which part of the country Jason couldn't fathom.

'Busy night?' he said uneasily, trying to make any sort of conversation to keep his thoughts on the straight and narrow.

'Very busy. In fact you might say it's been absolute murder,' she said, a smile turning up the corners of her mouth. 'But considering this is my first night as a cab driver I think I'm doing pretty well.'

'Your first night? Really?' said Jason with surprise. 'Well, just be careful who you pick up. There are a lot of strange characters around here. You never know what they might try if they see an attractive woman on her own, especially at night.'

'Oh, don't worry about me, Jason. I'm a big girl and very capable of looking after myself I can assure you,' she said with confidence while keeping her eyes firmly fixed on the road ahead.

'You know who I am?' said Jason, a little taken aback that she had called him by his first name.

'Everyone knows who you are around here, Mr Jason Worrall,' she raised an eyebrow, 'even if you've forgotten.'

'Yeah, quite the celebrity, aren't I?' muttered Jason, fixing his eyes on the falling snow.

'You were,' replied the woman.

An extended silence followed until it was finally broken by Jason. 'And like I was saying, just be careful. It makes no

57

difference how tough or streetwise you think you are, this is a rough neighbourhood, especially for a woman... dressed the way you are. Someone might get the wrong impression.'

'Don't you like the way I'm dressed, Jason?' she enquired with a smile. 'Anyway, what makes you so sure I don't want to give someone the wrong impression?'

Jason swallowed hard and seemed lost for words. It was clear that he was a little surprised by the woman's forward comments but it was also very clear from his expression that he was flattered by her teasing manner.

'You should be more careful that you don't end up cheating yourself out of money as well,' he said trying to change the tone of the conversation by pointing to the meter that she had forgotten to switch on when she picked him up.

'Oh, don't worry about the fare, Jason. This ride is on me.' She took an unexpected left turn off the main road and pulled the car up beside the gates of an abandoned breaker's yard filled with piles of scrapped cars covered in snow.

'Why have we stopped here?' he asked in confusion.

'Listen, I have a confession to make,' she said adopting a more serious tone, undoing her seat belt and switching off the engine.

'And what might that be?' Jason was curious.

'You know that I said this is my first night as a taxi driver?' he nodded.

'Well, I wasn't exactly telling you the truth,' she said twisting a strand of her hair round a finger.

'What do you mean?' Jason noticed how restless she seemed.

'What I mean is, I'm not really a taxi driver and this cab doesn't even belong to me.'

'Well, if you're not a taxi driver how are you riding about in one picking up passengers? Don't tell me you stole it?' Jason chuckled.

'Not exactly stole... I'd say more like borrowed... only the person I borrowed it from won't be having much use for it any more.'

Jason searched her face for some sort of clue to as what she meant but her expression betrayed no emotion and soberness overcame him as he realised she wasn't kidding.

'Who are you... really?

'My name is Lori,' said the woman, reaching into the side pocket of her door and pulling out a folded newspaper. 'But I think the papers have a different name for me.'

He carefully unfolded the paper and gazed at the front page story to see the headline FUTURE ASSASSIN KILLS AGAIN! It was the same story from the paper that Rachel had left for him to read that very morning. Jason stared at the story open-mouthed before looking back at the woman sitting next to him and he began to laugh.

'So what you're telling me is that you're the Future Assassin?'

'I'd prefer to be called the crime traveller, but unfortunately the name was already taken by a lousy TV show from the nineties,' Lori sighed.

'Well you certainly don't match your description.'

'Don't judge a book by its cover, Jason. People are not always what they appear to be, you should know that better than anyone.'

'Listen, I appreciate you trying to humour me but I'm not really in the mood so, if it's all the same to you, I'd just like you to take me home.'

'Look, I know this is hard for you to believe but I really am the Future Assassin,' said Lori in desperation.

'You know what? I think I'll walk the rest of the way.' Jason pulled on the door handle only to find it locked. 'Will you open this door, please?'

'Ok, but first let me prove to you that I'm telling you the truth,' Lori pleaded while Jason tried every button on the door in an attempt to unlock it. 'Take a look in the back seat... you'll see my black cloak and my gun along with a notebook that has detailed information from the future inside it.'

Jason let out a heavy sigh before taking a quick look at the back seat. A black cloak was thrown carelessly to one side with a tattered old book sticking out from underneath just as Lori had said. But there wasn't a gun in sight. He was about to turn back in his seat when something unexpected caught his eye. On the floor, barely visible among some empty soda cans and cigarette packs, he noticed the identity card of the person who looked as though he might be the true owner of the cab.

But before he could even think about reaching down to pick it up and quiz Lori on who it belonged to and what exactly it was doing on the floor, a heavy object made contact with the side of his face knocking him unconscious and turning the night that he thought couldn't get any worse into something a whole lot worse than he could ever have imagined.

CHAPTER 5 - A TIME TO KILL

It was the night of the party... that's the way the dream always began. And, as usual, Jason found himself standing outside the hall dressed in the same clothes he was wearing before the dream started while the sound of music and laughter echoed into the cold night air.

Suddenly, the sight of Jessica and Leona getting into Harry's car caught his attention and in panic he ran towards them, calling out their names, trying to warn them of the danger before it was too late. But they couldn't hear his voice any more than they could see his hands tapping against the window as the car's engine started and the heartbroken man at the wheel pulled away. Jason raced past and in a desperate act threw himself in front of the car hoping he could stop them from leaving and save them from their fate. But the car passed right through him as if he was nothing more than the ghost of a man.

Then the street where he stood disappeared and he found himself standing in the middle of a familiar scene surrounded by a large police presence that was diverting the traffic away from the closed-off road. A police helicopter flew low overhead towards the flashing blue and red lights of several emergency vehicles that were illuminating a smoke-covered area. Jason ran towards the lights, coughing in the petrol fumes and black smoke until he reached the scene of the accident. Firemen were trying to put out the flames on the cargo lorry that had turned on its side after the collision, while the ambulance team rushed its driver to their vehicle on a stretcher. But Harry's car was nowhere in sight and Jason broke down until he heard the voice of a little girl calling him and felt a small hand slip into his and grip it tightly. 'Please, Daddy, don't be upset,' said the voice of his daughter, as he turned and saw with horror her face smiling up at him through badly burnt skin. With a scream of terror he was abruptly torn from the dream and catapulted back to reality.

He woke with a start and blinked at the sun shining directly onto his face, believing for a few seconds that he must somehow have made it safely home after his strange encounter with Lori the night before. That is until he realised that his hands were bound tightly together behind his seat where he had been cramped up all night. He had a sore head, stiff neck and aching legs, and realised that the beautiful woman who had persuaded him to join her in the car where he was now imprisoned, was still sat next to him in the driver's seat, watching him with an amused look on her face.

'I wouldn't bother trying to escape if I were you,' said Lori, sipping a cup of coffee and smiling at the sight of Jason attempting to free his hands from the ropes. 'I tied those myself. Houdini wouldn't find his way out of those knots, I made sure of that.'

'Listen, lady, I don't know who you are or why you're doing this but you have to untie me.'

'You know exactly who I am, Jason. I told you that last night. And if you're wondering why your hands a tied behind the seat, well, it's for my own protection.' Lori filled her cup with the remains of the coffee in her flask. 'It's not like I had much choice in the matter. I mean let's face it, a man of your skills against a young girl like me...? I wouldn't stand a chance if you were to try something.'

'But I don't understand what all this is about... Where are we? Why have you brought me here?' Jason was looking out of the window seeing that they were parked near to a snow-covered farm cottage surrounded by fields looking like something straight off a Christmas card.

'If you must know we're in Accrington,' said Lori before taking another sip of her coffee.

'Accrington?' said Jason in disbelief.

'I know, I'm as shocked as you are. Thought we were never going to make it here by the way it was coming down last night. Still, at least it's cleared up now,' she said gazing up at the clear blue sky.

'Wait... what happened to the taxi cab you picked me up in?' he asked, realising that they were in a completely different car.

'Are you joking?' laughed Lori. 'Do you honestly think I'm going to drive around in some dead guy's cab? I torched that thing inside the breaker's yard where we stopped last night, after I took the owner's body out of the boot and put him in the driver's seat of course. Had to make it look like an accident… it's always better to make it look like an accident. Can't always go round shooting people.'

Jason stared at her before daring to speak. 'So that's why we're here,' he said in a low voice. 'You killed that poor cab driver and now you're going to kill me.'

'Well, I suppose that's one good reason why a crazed assassin would bring you out to the middle of nowhere.' Lori laughed and almost choked on her coffee.

'Yeah, well if that's what you intend to do then just get it over with. You'll be doing me a favour.'

'Aww, don't care about yourself, do you, Jase?' She placed her cup on the dashboard so she could wipe off the splashes of coffee that had spilled onto her legs. 'Because you think you have nothing to live for… but you're forgetting all about your parents and your best friend, the Golden Girl, the one who comes to visit you once a week to make sure you're doing alright.'

'So you've been spying on me too?'

Lori smirked.

'You leave them out of this.'

'Oh, don't worry; I'm going to, she replied reassuringly. 'I just can't help but wonder how they'd all feel if one morning they were to wake up to the awful news that the body of their beloved Jason was found floating in a lake, looking like he'd committed suicide. Now, you may not care about yourself anymore, Jason, but you care about your parents and you care about your little friend, so for that reason you're going to do exactly as I say or none of them will ever see you alive again. Ah, there's no blackmail like emotional blackmail, is there?'

'How can I believe you? How can I know for sure that you're not going to kill me just like you killed that poor taxi driver?' he demanded.

'Because that so-called poor taxi driver was about to chase a customer down a dark alleyway and beat him to death with a wheel brace for trying to escape without paying the fare. Luckily for him I was there to intervene.' Lori reached into the back seat for her book. 'Now written inside here from the first page to the last is detailed information from the future.' She flicked through the worn pages filled with poorly hand-written notes. 'Don't believe me? Take a look for yourself. It's all here; dates, times, names and places of wherever a mindless act of murder is about to take place. My job is merely to prevent these things from happening and save innocent people from a terrible fate.'

She waved the tattered book in front of Jason's face before closing it with a snap and throwing it into the back seat again. 'So you see, I only kill people whose names are in the book; people who are destined to kill someone else. Your name, however, is not in the book, because the only person you're in danger of killing is yourself with your very silly habit of mixing anti-depressants with two litres of scotch every night. I have no reason to kill you, Jason, not unless you give me one, so if you do exactly as I say you won't get hurt. Understood?'

'Then why are you doing this to me?' he asked seeming a little relieved. 'And why have you brought me here?

'For the company I suppose,' replied Lori, her eyes shining with humour. 'It gets a little lonely travelling to all these destinations on my own. It'll be nice to have someone to talk to and share my adventures with for a change. And it's not like you'd be doing anything else, is it, other than locking yourself away from the world so you can drink yourself into an early grave.'

'But what exactly are we doing parked up in this place?'

'Neighbours at war,' said Lori taking another sip of her coffee. 'A fight broke out a few years back between the elderly couple who own that lovely cottage over there and their not-so-friendly neighbour from the next farm who's been trying to build on land that the courts say legally is not his to build on.'

'So what's that got to do with you? Why don't you just let the courts deal with it?'

'Well, because the neighbour has taken the couple to court on several occasions and each time he's ended up with the same disappointing result. So, this morning, for whatever reason, he finally decides enough is enough and takes the law into his own hands by making his way through the field, sneaking his way onto their property and setting fire to the cottage, burning them both alive while they are sound asleep upstairs in their bedroom,' said Lori, acting as if such things were an everyday occurrence.

'That's ridiculous. How on earth could you have all this information? 'What...? are you from the future... have you got some kind of time machine that's transported you here?'

Lori rolled her eyes heavenward. 'Jason, do you honestly think that if I had a time machine that could transport me to any place I wanted at whatever time I chose that I'd be driving around in this old rust bucket?'

'What then? Do you have psychic powers... or premonitions, and write it all down inside that book?'

'Psychic powers? Me? Give over,' she replied, laughing at the very notion. 'Although it's funny you should say that because my granny was a fortune teller.'

'Well, how else can you know all this stuff?'

'If I told you would you believe me?'

'Probably not.'

'Well then, why should I waste my breath explaining anything more to you?' She shrugged her shoulders. 'Besides, I probably wouldn't believe me either if I were in your shoes so maybe it's better you find that out for yourself.'

Jason was about to say something in reply when the sight of a figure in the distance slowly making its way through the snow in the next field caught his attention. And it didn't take him long to realise that the stout-looking figure approaching was indeed the very man that Lori had predicted would arrive, carrying what looked like a gasoline can in one hand and a bag of something in the other.

'That's him,' said Lori, throwing the rest of her coffee out of the window and starting up the car. 'We'd better get out of sight before he spots us.' She reversed the car quietly around the side of a ramshackle stable with a rickety roof ready to collapse under the pressure of the snow.

'This is impossible,' said Jason as Lori switched off the engine and reached into the back seat for her cloak.

'Believe me now?' she said as she opened her door and got out, her sheepskin boots sinking into the snow as she quickly tied her hair into a pony tail and slipped on the cloak. 'Don't even think about calling for help, Jason.' She peered through a narrow slit in the stable wall. The scruffily-dressed man bobbed under a barbed-wire fence and onto the neighbour's land, the sound of empty bottles clinking together from the bag he was carrying as he made his way towards the cottage. 'If that man gets a glimpse of us hiding out here it won't be the cottage he petrol bombs it'll be the car, so keep it shut.'

'But wait... what are you going to do?' Concern showed in Jason's voice.

'What do you think I'm gonna do?' replied Lori, as she reached over him to open the glove compartment and pulled out a Magnum revolver. 'I'm going to change the future.' She smiled before covering her eyes and nose with the hood of her cloak and slamming her door shut; she looked every bit the grim reaper as she followed the man who had already disappeared round the side of the building.

Jason waited until Lori was out of sight before trying to free his hands from the ropes once again, but just as she had warned him there was no escaping no matter how hard he tried. Giving up the struggle he looked around for any sharp objects lying around in the car that might be within his reach. But the car was devoid of any such object that could be of use to him and, in frustration, he repeatedly hit his head against the back of the seat in which he was imprisoned, and with an exhausted sigh turned his face to the window. A robin had landed on the wing mirror next to him, watching as if it had deliberately come down to gloat at his misfortune and remind him of how good it felt to be free as a bird.

The sound of a gunshot broke the quiet of the morning, startling him and sending the brazen robin flying for the safety of some nearby trees. A panic-stricken Jason tried to free his hands once more, friction from the ropes burning his skin as he struggled to work his way through the countless knots. In one last bid, he placed both feet against the dashboard hoping that if he could push the seat back with enough force it would break under the pressure, loosening the ropes and setting him free.

But before he could even think about thrusting himself backwards Lori reappeared in front of the car, the sound of barking drawing nearer as she stopped momentarily to catch her breath before taking a quick glance over her shoulder, running round to the driver's door and sliding back into her seat.

'There's a big dog on the loose. It's chased me all the way from the cottage,' she gasped. She slammed her door shut just as a large Alsatian came charging round the corner and almost caught up with her.

'We've gotta get outta here before someone sees us,' she said as she struggled to get the keys into the ignition.

'I heard a gunshot... what did you do?' said Jason, almost jumping out of his skin at the sight of the dog's large paws against his window, spit spraying all over the glass as it snarled and barked furiously flashing a lethal set of yellow teeth.

'No time for explanations,' replied Lori, starting up the engine and crunching it into first gear. 'We've gotta get outta here now.'

A plume of snow sprayed up from the back wheels as they spun without moving the car. 'Oh shit! We're stuck,' said Lori turning to Jason and checking that she'd disengaged the handbrake. 'Jason, what are we going to do? I can't get out and clear the snow away, that bleeding great dog will have me for breakfast!'

The engine revved loudly as she put her foot flat to the floor and gripped the steering wheel tightly while rocking back and forth in her seat in a futile effort to get the car moving. 'Come on, you stupid piece of crap… you're gonna get us caught,' she yelled as if the car could understand her, before punching the steering wheel and accidentally sounding the horn.

'Turn the wheel and go easy on the gas,' Jason instructed leaning closer to Lori in fear that the dog would find its way through the glass at any moment. She did as Jason ordered and sure enough the car began to move forward, swaying from side to side as it appeared from its hiding place, gaining momentum along the driveway that could easily have passed for an ice rink. The dog ran alongside biting at the wheel.

Lori adjusted her rear view mirror and let out a sigh of relief as she took a fleeting glance at the farm cottage and saw that the shutters were still closed in the bedroom window and the inhabitants were nowhere to be seen. A Cheshire cat grin came over her face as the car shot back onto the road, scraping past the gate that she had busted open on the way in, before disappearing onto the narrow lane that led back to the main road leaving behind a cloud of smoke from the exhaust.

A plastic bag drifted through the air as the dog ran back towards the cottage, its nose pressed firmly to the ground, sniffing curiously at the patches of red snow trailing around the side of the house, until it came to the body of the man, lying face down in the snow in a pool of his own blood with the petrol can still gripped tightly in his hand.

The dog whimpered and moaned momentarily as it gazed at the plastic bag blowing back and forth in the morning breeze, before letting out a chilling howl over the dead man's carcass.

*

'Phew, that was a close one,' said Lori, throwing back the hood of her cloak as they sped down the lane. 'Thanks for the tip, Jase. We'd probably never have made it out of there if it wasn't for your quick thinking.' She gave him a playful slap on the leg.

'I can't believe what you've done,' said Jason, still unable to make sense of the events he'd witnessed.

'Oh, relax will you. At least we're out of danger now.' Lori removed the hair band from her pony tail and allowed her hair to fall back over her shoulders.

'Relax? How can I relax?' 'You've just killed someone!'

'No, Jason, I've just saved two people's lives. There's a big difference.'

An untamed branch overhanging the road scraped against the roof, startling Jason and almost sending the car crashing into the hedgerow as Lori swerved to avoid it.

'You've got to see the bigger picture here.' Lori looked steadily at the road ahead. 'I'm not the villain in all this. That man's name was in the book. You saw for yourself what he was about to do.'

'I don't care if his name was in your stupid book. That didn't give you the right to kill him,' said Jason, his voice strained with anger. 'There must've been another way to stop him without anyone having to get hurt.'

'Oh, really? What would you suggest? I mean, what would a police community support officer have done in a situation like that?' asked Lori sarcastically, not giving him a chance to reply. 'Even if I were to intervene without harming him do you honestly think that he wouldn't try something like this again? Give me a break. There's only one way to deal with a scumbag like that and you just saw it.'

'This can't be happening to me.'

'Oh, it is happening, Jason, so you might as well get comfy in your seat because our little day out together is only just beginning,' said Lori with a huge smile.

'Wait... what is that supposed to mean?' A look of horror clouded Jason's face.

'Don't tell me you thought it was going to end there?' she laughed, clicked her tongue and shook her head. 'Sorry to disappoint you, Jason, but the book says that there are many more destinations we must visit today before the day is over.'

'You can't do this to me... I don't want to be part of this,' he demanded pulling on the ropes in a poor attempt to free his hands.

'Sorry, no can do,' replied Lori with the same cocky smile that hadn't quite left her face since Jason had stepped into the car with her. 'You're part of this now whether you like it or not, so there's no point in arguing.'

Jason rested his head against the window and flinched as he felt a sharp pain in the side of his face.

'Oh… erm… sorry about the wack I gave you last night,' she apologised as he leant over to the rear view mirror to check the bruising on his left cheek. 'It was nothing personal. I hope you understand.'

Jason turned and stared at Lori in total contempt as the car slowed and she took a sharp left onto the main road heading for the next destination.

CHAPTER 6 - KNOWLEDGE IS POWER

Christmas was fast approaching and the new retail store in Merseyside was aglow with crowds of people rushing to complete their present lists. Lori circled the crowded parking lot, huffing and puffing to herself in aggravation as she searched without success for a place to park before impatiently manoeuvring her car into a disabled bay with no regard for the driver behind who had to brake suddenly as she swooped in front of him

'See, this is why I hate this time of year, everyone pushing and shoving in front of one another with no patience whatsoever,' said Lori, acting as if the driver behind was the one in the wrong. 'Christmas is only one bloody week in the year. The way some of these idiots act anyone would think it was gonna last all year round.' She switched off the engine and stretched before reaching into the pocket of her jacket for her cigarettes.

'What on earth are we doing here?' Jason gazed ahead at the massive retail store heaving with Christmas shoppers all caught up in the festive spirit. 'This doesn't seem like a place where something bad could happen.'

'You'd be surprised,' she replied, a cigarette hanging from her lips as she searched the rest of her pockets for a light. 'Sometimes bad things can happen in places where you'd least expect them. This place is no exception. We are in Liverpool let's don't forget.'

'So what happens here?' he asked as Lori took a huge drag on her cigarette and blew a cloud of smoke out through her window. She glanced at her watch.

'Well, let's say... oh, in about ten minutes from now a man is going to walk out of that store with a five-year-old girl who's wandered away from her parents who are too busy choosing presents to notice. He's going to take her round the side of the store to a short cut that's been made through the steel fence leading to a street of council houses on the other side, and then he's going to take her away with him in his car.'

'What happens to the little girl?'

'Nobody ever finds out. She's never seen again and the man who abducts her is later charged with her murder.' Lori took another lungful of smoke.

'So what do you intend to do?' Jason asked the question to which he already knew the answer.

'Well, I'm going to save the little girl obviously. Any objections?'

'No... no, I haven't. If what you say is true then you should save her.'

'Why do I feel a 'but' coming?' said Lori, knowing what was on Jason's mind.

'But I don't agree with you killing her abductor. You can stop this from happening without anyone getting killed.'

'Oh, please, will you stop with all this goody-two-shoes nonsense.' Lori flicked her fag end out of the window. 'This man is a paedophile for crying out loud. If I don't stop him now who's to say that he won't try again with some other poor child in the near future. Do you want that to happen? Do you really want to put another innocent life on the line because of your stupid Christian values?'

'You have to see the bigger picture here,' Lori continued not giving Jason a chance to reply. 'Not only are we saving a little girl's life today but we're making sure no parent has to go through the heartache of losing their child at the hands of this pervert. I thought you of all people would understand... especially after losing your daughter.'

'Don't act like you know me.' Jason was angry. 'You know nothing about me.'

'What... you think you were just picked at random from the street? Trust me, Jason, I know everything about you,' said Lori smiling confidently. 'I know that you're a Salford lad born and bred, and after finishing school your dream was to become a police officer, until your best friend, Miss Butter Wouldn't Melt in Her Mouth, convinced you to join her in becoming a PCSO because it allowed you to interact with the community on a more local and personal level. I know that you're a natural leader and, despite your distaste for the spotlight, you always seem to find yourself centre stage. I also know that you earned yourself a medal for bravery for single-handedly stopping three armed and dangerous men from robbing a local post office filled with innocent bystanders, only to quit your duties as a PCSO after the deaths of your ex-wife and your daughter.'

Jason looked at Lori lost for words. Who was this strange woman who knew so much about his life, and, more importantly, what on earth did she want with him? 'If you know so much about my life then why didn't you do anything to help me?' he said, finally finding his voice.

'I don't understand.' Now it was Lori's turn to be confused.

'If you know so much about me, why didn't you save my family? Answer me that.'

Lori looked down and sighed. 'I'm sorry, I really am, but despite what you believe history shows that what happened to your family was an accident. It was out of my hands, there was nothing I could do.'

Jason let out a snort of humourless laughter and turned his head away.

'I'm sorry I couldn't help you then, but at least I'm trying to help you now.' Lori placed a hand on his shoulder to comfort him.

'Help me?' Jason was outraged. 'You've knocked me unconscious, kidnapped me, and now you're forcing me to accompany you on a killing spree! How on earth are you helping me?'

'Well at least you're not in the house drinking yourself senseless. Look, I don't think you fully appreciate the trouble I've put myself to just to have you here. It wasn't an easy task you know. It took a lot of plotting and working out before I could even think about making a move. You probably wouldn't be sitting next to me right now if I hadn't told that shop keeper not to serve you anymore alcohol.'

'Wait... that was you?'

'Yeah!' laughed Lori sounding like a naughty child. 'Although I have to admit I thought my plan was blown the moment you walked into the bar.'

'So, you were lurking around waiting for me to come out so you could pick me up? Is there anything else you did to make sure your little scheme went to plan?'

'Not really. Apart from when I went into your house after your little friend left so I could empty out that bottle of scotch I saw you stashing behind the cabinet. Well, I had to find a way to lure you out of that house of yours, didn't I? Of course you were too busy sleeping to catch me creeping in and out, and by the time you woke I was long gone.'

'But... how did you get in? The front door was locked.'

'Because you made the silly mistake of leaving the back door open. It was way too easy.'

'So, you've gone to all this trouble just to get me into your car, but what you still haven't explained to me is why?'

Lori was about to reply when she saw a man coming out of the store holding hands with a little girl. 'That's him,' she said pointing towards the rakish looking elderly gentleman, wearing a trilby hat and a brown tweed jacket, walking with a slight stoop as he led the smiling child around the corner.

'Wait now… what are you going to do? Jason tried not to panic. 'There must be CCTV cameras all over this place… you can't just go up to him and shoot him.'

'Don't worry, I've done my research.' Lori calmly reached into the back seat to retrieve her gun. 'As it happens, the only CCTV cameras in this place are the ones in the shop. All I have to do is catch up to old bendy legs before he reaches his car. Don't even need a cloak for this one.' She opened her revolver to check the chamber and discovered it was empty.

'You're probably wondering why I wait until the last minute to strike,' she said, searching in the side pocket of her door for the small see-through pouch where she kept her ammunition. 'I guess you're thinking, wouldn't it be easier just to kill the person before they can even get close to their intended victim. I guess I should really.' Lori stopped her search and looked at Jason thoughtfully: 'But it's kind of a personal thing. I just like to make sure that they really are going to do what the book foretells. Now, where have I put those bleedin bullets? They've got to be here somewhere.' She leant across Jason's lap to look inside the glove compartment.

'Big mistake,' he said, wrapping his leg around her in one swift move and pinning her in a headlock as if he were a professional wrestler.

'Jason, what are you doing?' Lori screamed, trying desperately to free herself. 'Let go of me, I don't want to hurt you,' she pleaded through muffled gasps.

'You're the one who's gonna get hurt if you don't stop struggling.' Jason pressed down hard with his leg in an effort to keep Lori from overpowering him until she finally managed to free her right arm and blindly reached for the taser inside her jacket, hesitated for a moment to get her aim in, then thrust it hard into Jason's hip.

He cried out in pain as Lori blasted him forcing him to release his grip and allow her to move back to her seat.

'You idiot,' she said, her cheeks flushed and her hair in a dishevelled mess as she leant her head back against the window to catch her breath. 'Are you trying to get that child killed?' She swapped the taser for the gun she'd dropped on the floor. 'What on earth were you thinking?' She grabbed the pouch of bullets out of the glove compartment, at the same time retrieving her flick knife, and quickly loaded her gun stowing both weapons in her jacket pockets. She checked through the window for any sign of the old man and the girl but they had already disappeared round the corner.

'Now, don't you even think about pulling a stunt like that again.' Jason was still recovering from the electricity passing through his body, the most painful moment of his life. 'Because if you even try alerting someone while I'm gone I won't think twice about putting a bullet in you or anyone else that stands in my way... understood?'

Leaving Jason immobilised in his seat, Lori left the car in a hurry and ran towards the corner of the store. The man and the girl were nowhere to be seen as she rounded the corner and headed towards the short cut that was barely visible at the far end of the chain link fence. She slipped through the man-made hole without a moment's hesitation, cursing under her breath as her clothing caught on the branches overhanging the narrow path, until she reached the far side and spotted the old man leading the girl to where his car was parked.

Lori raised the Magnum to take aim when she caught sight of a silver-haired woman standing by the door of a house across the road, waving fondly and calling out to the little girl as she and the elderly gentleman headed in her direction. Lori wasn't quite sure what to make of this but, judging by how comfortable the child was walking next to the old man as he guided her across the road, and seeing how excitedly she was waving back to the woman waiting to meet her, she realised that these two could not be the ones whose names were written in the book.

Knowing full well from her past experiences that the information in the book wasn't always accurate, Lori hung back to make sure no mistake was being made, but her suspicions were soon confirmed when she heard the little girl call out, 'Grandma, grandma' and saw her greet the woman with a big hug. The man took off his hat and complained that taking the short cut had not done his back any favours before following them inside the house and closing the door behind him.

'Shit!' said Lori, darting back through the short cut as quickly as she could and running at top speed to the front of the store, hiding her gun as she went. Looking all around her she began to panic, knowing full well that if the man had already left with the child there would be nothing she could do to help. The information in the book only gave the events that were going to take place, and apart from the names of the man and the girl with their descriptions, there were no other details that would be of any use.

By the entrance a man dressed in a green elf suit stood waiting holding a charity collecting box. 'Would you like to make a donation for homeless children at Christmas, miss?' he asked, shaking his collection box to get Lori's attention as she took a quick peek inside the store for any sign of the two people she sought.

'No, I wouldn't,' she snapped in frustration, about to retreat to the car when she noticed an elderly man making his way through the parking lot holding the hand of a crying child who seemed reluctant to walk with him. He was shorter and stouter than the book's description and, to anyone paying attention, the little girl's apparent desperation to return to the store only made her look like a spoiled brat giving her helpless grandfather a hard time for not buying her the present she wanted. To anyone except that is for Lori who knew with certainty that this was the man she was looking for. Her eyes narrowed as she watched him put the crying child in the back seat of his car, smiling and shaking his head at passers by before rushing round to the driver's side ready to make his escape.

'Now your mummy and daddy have asked me to look after you for a while so they can tell Santa what presents you want,' said the man, taking off his hat and adjusting his rear view mirror so he could see the sobbing child who looked too terrified to move. 'So in the meantime, me and you are going for a little ride together until they're ready to pick you up. Ok?' he smiled, ready to start the car and take the girl away when, without warning, the passenger door opened and Lori got in.

'Don't even think about making a move,' she said to the startled old man, the gun in her left hand pointed directly at him as she reached into the back to open the door for the girl. 'Emily sweetie, I want you to go back to the store and wait there by the entrance until your parents come and find you and don't you ever wander away from them again, do you understand?'

The girl nodded her head, pushed open the door and got out of the car, not once looking back as she hurried along the pedestrian walkway towards the store.

'What is the meaning of all this?' the old man gasped, his hands raised in surrender.

Lori waited until the girl had vanished from view before turning her attention to him. 'Don't play the innocent with me, Mr Richard Ocamp. I know this isn't the first time you've tried something like this, but I promise you today is going to be the last.'

The old man braced himself waiting for Lori to pull the trigger but there was no gunshot. Instead, he felt as though someone had punched him hard in the chest as she retrieved her flick knife from a pocket and with a steady hand thrust it hard into his rib cage.

'Now, I don't have time to give you the slow death you deserve,' Lori whispered into his ear as she twisted the blade deeper into the wound. 'So I'll just have to make do with a really painful one instead.'

She watched as the man gurgled in pain, the grimace of agony on his face morphing into a blank stare. Blood leaked from the corner of his mouth, running down the deeply wrinkled cheek into his beard, and he breathed his last even before Lori could remove the knife.

*

'You know I would never have touched you with that taser if you hadn't acted so stupid back there.' Lori glanced at Jason with a guilty expression as they sped along the motorway.

'What were you thinking going all WWE on me like that?' The sound of Jason's moans and groans from the after effects cut through her like a knife.

'Although it's probably for the best that you did because you stopped me from making a huge mistake,' she added, as if that was any vindication.

Jason gave her a look of disgust before closing his eyes and leaning his head against the window, hoping to ease his discomfort.

'Oh Jase, don't look at me like that. I've said I'm sorry haven't I. What more can I say? It's not as if I had any choice in the matter.' She sighed, realising that her apologies were getting her nowhere. 'Look, you must be starving. How about we stop at the next services and grab a bite to eat?' she said, hoping that this would change his mood.

Jason did not respond, but continued to moan quietly to himself with his head still resting against the window.

'Come on, Jason. We've got a long way to go... you might as well get something inside you. It might even ease the pain a little too.'

'What do you mean, we have a long way to go? How much longer do you intend keeping me here? You have to untie me, the ropes are cutting into my wrists,' he added.

'Aww Jase, you know I can't do that just yet, especially after the stunt you pulled back there. I can't take the risk. But if you do exactly as I say, very soon you'll be free of the ropes.'

Lori turned the car off the motorway and headed for the service station.

*

After finding a quiet place to park away from the other cars and the HGVs and coaches that spread into almost every corner of the large service area, Lori used her hip to push open the exit door of the Welcome Break café, carrying two soft drinks inside a tray with one hand and a huge bag of fast food with the other. As she headed back to her car a series of wolf whistles greeted her from every direction from drivers who stuck their heads out of the windows of their vehicles, honked their horns in delight and shouted tasteless remarks as she passed.

'Oh, piss off, you greasy bunch of retards! Lori spat, unable to hold back her temper at the offensive comments to which she was being subjected. She didn't once look back until she reached her Ford Focus, which had gained many more dents and scrape marks covering the metallic paintwork since the previous day.

'Dirty pervs!' she muttered as she put the tray and the brown paper bag on the roof so she could open the door. 'Now, I hope you're hungry, Mr Worrall, because I've got us a right gut filler here.'

Lori slipped into her seat and placed the drinks and the hot paper bag on the dashboard, only to find that her passenger had dozed off. A tender smile appeared on her face as she watched him sleep. Despite his messy hair and scruffy stubble that gave him the appearance of a homeless person, there was still a handsome face to be admired and she found herself wishing that she could abandon her duties for the day and spend the rest of the afternoon getting to know him better.

'Aww, you get some rest, babe,' she said softly as she gently moved his head into a more comfortable position against the head rest. 'We have a long road ahead of us… I'll wake you when we get there.'

CHAPTER 7 - ANOTHER TIME, ANOTHER PLACE

'Jason... wakey, wakey... time to get up,' said Lori quietly, trying to wake him with a little tug on the hood of his coat and a gentle tap to his cheek.

'What... where... where are they?' Jason slowly came out of his unconscious state and opened his eyes to see Lori staring at him curiously. 'I thought I saw them... I thought they were...' Unable to separate his dreams from reality he gazed around drowsily.

'What on earth are you talking about? You were just dreaming, you dinlo.' Lori reached for the soft drink she'd saved for him in the cup holder. 'Here, have a sip of this, it'll make you feel better.' She held the drink up to his face putting the straw to his lips. 'Don't worry, it's not poison.' She rolled her eyes as Jason looked at her suspiciously, before sucking on the straw until the cup was empty.

'Good Lord you were thirsty! We'd better save this in case you need the toilet later,' said Lori, placing the paper cup back into the holder. 'There are some fries and pieces of boneless chicken in that bag if you're hungry, although they're probably stone cold by now.'

'How long have I been out?'

'Must be at least three hours.' Lori reached into a pocket for a cigarette. 'You slept like a baby the whole way.'

'What do you mean the whole way? Where are we?' said Jason, taking in his surroundings and seeing that it was now dark outside apart from the light of a full moon. They were in the car park of a church opposite a hotel with a huge sign on its wall reading BLANCO'S HOTEL AND RESTAURANT and an arrow beneath directing customers to the parking lot round the side of the building.

'Tell me where we are?' he demanded taking in the parish building on one side and the hotel across the road where disco lights flashed through the frosted glass windows and loud party music echoed into the quiet streets.

'Haven't you noticed the beautiful mountains?' Lori blew a little cloud of smoke out of her window and gazed at the mountains that overlooked the town shimmering in the moonlight. 'There's only one place I know where mountains look so wonderful at this time of year and that's South Wales.'

'South Wales? Why have you driven us all the way down to South Wales?' asked Jason in disbelief.

'Are you sure you want to know? I mean you're not going to go all WWE on me again if I tell you?' Lori's voice dripped with sarcasm.

'If it's any consolation I'm not too happy about being here either. This place brings back a lot of memories for me. It was my family's favourite place to visit when we were on our travels. We even used to attend mass here every Sunday during our stay.' She turned her attention to the building next to them with a notice board at the front declaring it to be Saint Joseph's Catholic Church and giving the times of services for the week.

'I must have been about ten years old the last time I was here; I remember it as being so much bigger.'

'Family? You?' sneered Jason.

'Yes, Jase, I have a family too you know... well, at least I did once. I wasn't always this way, believe it or not, stealing money out of dead people's pockets and living in one cheap hotel after another. Before all of this I was just like any other girl with dreams of one day getting married and having children and living happily ever after... until suddenly it was all taken from me and, like you, I was left with nothing; nothing but an empty home as a constant reminder of all the things that could and should have been. You think you're the only one to have had your heart ripped out, to have had the people you care about most in the world taken from you by a mindless act? No, the dark and lonely road you find yourself on now is a road I've already travelled down and it's the road that led me here. So don't think for one minute that I wanted this life; I'm only playing the hand I was dealt.'

Jason watched Lori's face, listening to the sad tone in her voice as she unintentionally let down her defences showing him a more vulnerable side to her somewhat ruthless and carefree personality. Despite everything she had put him through in the short time since they had met, he found himself sympathising with her. The pain in her eyes and the hurt clouding her expression as she hinted at a story from her past that sounded not dissimilar to his own and made her seem more like a confused, frightened little girl.

'You still haven't told me why we're here.'

'Well, it's a bit early yet.' Lori looked at her watch. 'Driving from Liverpool to Port Talbot didn't take quite as long as I expected.'

'Early for what?'

'Well, let's say in about half an hour a man is going to stagger out of that hotel, stinking drunk from the works do that's going on there. He's then going to foolishly jump into his car and attempt to drive home, only to lose control somewhere along the way and end up mounting the pavement and mowing down a young couple who are walking home from a friend's house, killing them both instantly.'

Jason looked predictably stunned. 'Now wait a minute, if what you say is true then you can't kill this man.'

'And why not?' Lori flicked what was left of her cigarette out of the window and checked her teeth in the wing mirror.

'Because he's just a drunk driver... it's not exactly fair to label him as a killer.'

'Sorry, Jase, but a killer is a killer. This man is just as much a danger to society as all the other people I've taken out. I thought you of all people would know what the consequences are of driving dangerously.'

'Don't you even dare to compare this to what happened to my family. Harry's actions were calculated. This man is just making a stupid mistake that anyone, including you or me, could make,' said Jason, not letting his emotions get the better of him. 'And it's Christmas for crying out loud… there must be a hundred drunk drivers on the road tonight.'

'You're probably right, but their names aren't on the hit list.'

'But that still doesn't give you the right to kill him,' pleaded Jason. 'How many people have had too much to drink and think they're still sober enough to drive? It doesn't make you a bad person, just an irresponsible driver.'

'So what's your point,' said Lori, shrugging her shoulders.

'My point is you don't have to kill him. There's other ways to stop him from driving without anyone having to get hurt.'

'Like what?'

Jason stared thoughtfully at the hotel across the road. 'Let me speak to him. I can talk him out of getting into his car, I know I can.'

'What! Are you being serious?' Lori laughed. 'Do you honestly think I'm going to risk letting you out of this car so you can go and talk some old drunk out of driving home? What do you take me for?'

'I didn't ask you to let me out of the car. You can park next to his and I'll talk to him from my window.'

'And just say I was to do what you want and you somehow manage to talk him into handing over his keys, who's to say that he won't try the exact same thing on a different night and end up killing some other poor soul?' Lori was unconvinced.

'That's just speculation, Lori. We'll never know unless we try,' said Jason hoping to appeal to her better nature, if she had one.

Lori came to a decision. 'Ok... let's give it a try, but I warn you now he's not gonna listen.'

'He will. I was a community support officer once, remember? I used to deal with this sort of stuff all the time,' said Jason with a sigh of relief.

'Then let's just hope for his sake that you haven't lost your touch,' said Lori, drawing a long breath as she started the car and headed for the hotel car park.

*

Some time later, a round-faced, plump man dressed in a Santa Claus costume staggered his way out of Blanco's hotel just as Lori had predicted. Intoxicated on a mixture of champagne and punch, his fake white beard and moustache pulled under his chin, he sang along to a well-known Christmas song that was blaring from the party which was still in full swing. Unsteadily he made his way to where his car was parked.

'Here comes Santa, Jase, better get into character,' said Lori, seeing the man approaching in her wing mirror.

'Just stay quiet and let me do the talking, ok?'

Lori pressed the button on her door to open the passenger window. 'Don't worry I won't say a word, but remember we haven't got all night. You have five minutes to get those keys off him... I don't think I need to go into detail about what will happen if you fail.'

The man stopped and leant against the side of his car to search his pockets for the car keys before standing up and stumbling towards the driver's door.

Jason stuck his head out of the window and put on his best voice of authority. 'Erm... excuse me, sir... I don't think it's a good idea for you to be driving now, is it?'

The drunk kept his back to Jason humming the rest of the song he'd been singing along to as he fumbled around with his keys trying to figure out which of them was the correct one to unlock the doors. He only became aware of Jason's presence after Lori honked her horn to get his attention. The man wobbled sideways and looked startled.

'I said I don't think it's a good idea for you to be driving now, is it, sir?' Jason repeated.

'Really? And what makes you say that?' the man replied, struggling to regain his balance.

Jason glanced at Lori before answering. 'Look, why don't you just do the sensible thing and get a taxi home? You can easily come back tomorrow for your car when your senses have returned.'

'Now, listen here, Boyo,' said the man with a slur in his strong Welsh accent as he moved closer to Jason's window. 'I'm quite cap... capable of driving home... if it's any business of yours.'

'Come on now, sir, I think we both know that isn't true.' Jason turned his head away having got a whiff of the man's alcohol-fumed breath.

'No one knows an alcoholic like another alcoholic,' Lori's voice dripped with sarcasm.

'You get into that car tonight and I promise you'll be spending the best part of the Christmas holidays inside a prison cell.' Jason faced the man once more.

'You're not a policeman, are you?' said the man with a curious expression.

'Not exactly... I'm a... I mean... We're... police community support officers.' Lori sniggered.

'Are you sure about that? You don't look like a police... thingy to me,' said the drunk, eyeing Jason suspiciously. 'I mean let's face it, you're not even wearing a uniform or... or a badge or anything...You're not even in the right car.'

'Time's running out, Jason,' Lori whispered, putting on the pressure.

'No… that's because we're… off duty,' said Jason, cringing at the poor excuse. 'Now, why don't you do the right thing and hand over your car keys. You're going to land yourself in a hell of a lot of trouble if you don't.'

'That's the understatement of the year,' added Lori

The man's eyes widened as he stared at Jason, hiccoughing loudly before speaking. 'No… no… now I know I might be a little tipsy but I'm not stupid… and I'm sure you're just saying all this to stop me from driving. Thanks for your concern but I really should be getting back, the wife won't be too happy if I'm home late.'

'No, please sir, listen to me. Don't get into that car; you're making a huge mistake.' The drunk turned his back and began to fiddle with his car keys again.

'Time's up… I've had enough of this crap,' said Lori as she got out of her car and headed towards the other one.

'Now, Mr Nicholas, my good friend Jason has asked you nicely to hand over your keys, so are you going to do what he asks?' Lori threw her arm across the man's shoulder and beckoned him to the front of his car where a small crash barrier edged the car park to prevent vehicles from running down the steep slope leading to the river at the bottom.

'Listen, my lovely... I appreciate your friend's concern but I promise you I'm fine... I'm sober as a judge,' the man insisted delighted by the young woman's presence.

'See, Jason, I told you he wouldn't listen.'

The drunk clutched her, getting a bit too close for comfort. 'Here... how's about me and you going on a little sleigh ride together? I might even let you sit on Santa's knee if you're a good little girl.' He snorted with laughter, abandoning all thoughts of his poor wife at home in favour of this dark-haired temptress.

Lori removed the man's hands from her waist and took a step back. 'Sorry, Santa, I might be a lot of things, but a good little girl isn't one of them.'

With a wicked smile she lunged forward, tipping the man over the crash barrier, and sending him rolling all the way down the slope to the very edge of the river bank. Lori smiled to herself as she gazed at the drunk's unmoving body before turning back to Jason.

'Lori, noooo!' Jason shouted, sticking his head out of the window and looking for any sign of the man, but all he could see was his Santa hat on the ground by Lori's feet and hear the sound of the fast-flowing river below.

'What have you done? You've killed him,' he said in despair.

'Keep your voice down, you tit!' said Lori, glancing around to make sure no one had witnessed her actions, before casually walking back to her car.

'Let me out of here, I can save him.' Jason battled with the ropes around his wrists as Lori slipped back into her seat.

'Will you be quiet,' said Lori, starting up the car and pressing the button to close the passenger window.

'You have to let me out, we can't just leave him,' pleaded Jason.

'There's no point, Jase, he's dead… and if he isn't now then he soon will be.' Gears crunched as she put the car into reverse before speeding out of the car park onto the main road.

'You didn't need to do that; I almost had those keys off him.'

'Oh, don't talk rubbish, he would've never given you those keys, I knew that from the start,' Lori answered in a cruel, calm voice.

'Then why did you even bother to let me talk to him?'

'Because I thought it might shut you up if you saw how stubborn the guy was.'

'But there was no need to do what you did. You could've easily taken the keys from him, you didn't have to push the poor man to his death.'

'Look, it's like I told you before, if I'd have let him live he would only have done the same thing to someone else... another time another place where I wouldn't have been able to stop him... so, chin up and take comfort from the fact that we've just saved two people's lives.'

'Stop saying we. I've told you I don't want to be part of this.'

'Shame you still feel that way, because I think we make a pretty good team.' Lori sighed.

There was silence for a moment as Jason looked at her curiously. 'So that's it... that's what this is all about. You want me to join you.'

'Hooray, he's finally got it,' said Lori, quirking an eyebrow.

'Are you serious? Do you honestly think I'm going to join you in killing people?'

'No, Jase. I want you to join me in saving people. Didn't I tell you to look at the bigger picture? Today alone we've prevented an elderly couple from being burnt to death in their home, we've stopped a little girl from being taken away by a paedophile, and we've saved a pair of newly-weds from being killed by a drunk driver. Just imagine what we could do if we worked together every day,' said Lori with a beaming smile.

'No, you did all that. I was just forced to witness it.'

'You helped me when the car was trapped in the snow,' Lori reminded him, 'and you stopped me from killing the wrong person at the retail store... even if it was unintentional.'

'This is crazy,' Jason laughed.

'Look, I know kidnapping you and tying you to a seat isn't exactly a good way to try and convince you to join me, but it was the only option I had to let you see all of this for yourself and understand that I'm telling you the truth. I'm not gonna lie to you, I'm in this way over my head and I can't do it on my own any more. I need help, and who better to help me than a man with your credentials? Jason, you were chosen above everyone else because you single-handedly stopped three armed men from robbing a post office full of innocent bystanders... how many other people could do that?'

Jason looked out of the window and Lori knew that she was treading on thin ice by brining up his past.

'Look, I know you're hurt and I know you've had your heart broken... believe me, we both have... but you don't have to be alone anymore. Join me and together we can make sure that no one else ever has to go through the horrors that we have. Me and you, Jase, we're the same. You know how it feels to have an entire community depending on you to clean up their streets, because they're either too scared or too lazy to do it for themselves, and like me you know how it feels to lose the people that are most precious to you.'

'We're not the same. I never killed anyone.' Jason kept his head turned to the window.

'Fair enough… but let me ask you this… if you could go back to the night before your wife and daughter were killed, knowing then what you know now, are you telling me that you wouldn't stop Harry from taking their lives? Even if the only option was to kill him?'

Lori's question met with no reply. 'Of course you would. You'd do whatever was necessary to guarantee their safety… and that's all I'm doing, only for other people, not myself… and all I'm asking is for you to help me. You and I have nothing left, Jason, but together we can make a difference in the world. So, what do you say?'

A short silence followed until at last Jason spoke. 'Do me a favour, please… don't talk to me for the rest of the journey.' He glanced at Lori before returning to the darkness beyond his window.

'Fine… suit yourself,' she said in disappointment as she turned the car onto the slip road and re-joined the motorway.

CHAPTER 8 - TIME WILL TELL

'Come on, Jason, this is childish. How long are you going to keep this up? You haven't spoken to me for nearly two hours!' said Lori in frustration. She pulled the car up by the kerb next to a small block of flats where a group of teenagers were messing around in a playground nearby.

'You can't keep this up all night, you're gonna have to speak to me sooner or later.' She sighed, glancing at the rowdy group of kids who were laughing hysterically as they took it in turns to knock back gulps from a large bottle of alcohol.

'Didn't I tell you not to speak to me?' Jason finally answered. The lights from the Christmas decorations in the windows of the flats shone down on the car allowing him to see a ghostly reflection of Lori's face in his window. 'I've got nothing more to say to you so don't waste your breath.'

'But aren't you the least bit interested in why we're parked up in this grotty council estate in Bristol?'

'No, I don't care. I just want you to take me home.'

'Oh, I think you will care about this one, trust me.'

Jason turned slowly to face her. 'And what is that supposed to mean?'

'I thought you didn't care,' Lori smirked nodding at the gang of noisy teenagers. 'See those kids over there? Well, they're from the estate next door and the only reason they're hanging around these parts tonight is because they're waiting for a sixteen-year-old girl to come out of that block of flats. They've been bullying her for several months and when she appears in about ten minutes time they intend to attack her.'

Jason looked more shocked than ever before as his eyes shifted from the menacing gang of teenagers back to Lori. 'What? They intend to kill her?'

'Well, I wouldn't be here otherwise, would I?'

'And what are you planning to do?' said Jason, although he thought he already knew the answer to his own question.

'Do I have to spell it out, Jase?'

'But, Lori… you can't kill them, they're only kids. Surely there's another way to stop them?'

'I knew you were going to say that,' Lori chuckled. '"Lori, you can't do this… Lori, you can't do that…" that's all I've heard out of you from the moment you woke up this morning. You should know what the rules are by now.'

'Listen to me!' demanded Jason. 'This is different; we're not dealing with adults here. We're just dealing with a bunch of kids. Surely even you can't harm children?'

'I'm sorry, Jase, there's no other way,' said Lori, acting as if she had a conscience.

'But there is a way, Lori, there's always a way... Let me speak to them. Let me speak to them and I promise I'll stop them from harming the girl. That way, no one will get killed.'

'You said that last time and that didn't work out too well, did it?' Lori was unconvinced.

'It'll be different this time but only if you let me do it my way.'

'And what exactly does your way mean?'

Jason took a deep breath before answering. 'Well, you're going to have to untie these ropes so that I can walk over there and speak to them.'

Lori burst out laughing. 'Aww, nice try, Jason... as if I'd be stupid enough to fall for that.'

'I won't try anything, I promise, if that's what you're worried about.'

'Sorry, Jase, but you know I can't trust you. We both know that if I untie you, you're gonna make a run for it and you'll end up making me do something I really don't want to.'

'I won't, I give you my word. You're the one with gun. If I was to do a runner I know I'd get myself killed as well as those kids. I don't want that, I just want to help them.'

Jason continued to beg as Lori folded her arms and shook her head.

'Come on, Lori, what do you have to lose? You're the one who's dragged me here to see all this… how can you even expect me to consider joining you if you won't prove to me that there's no other way to prevent all these things from happening?

'What? So if I can prove to you that there is no other way of stopping this gang from harming that girl tonight, you'll consider joining me?'

Jason shrugged his shoulders. 'Well, everything else you've tried so far hasn't worked.'

Lori turned her attention to the teenagers as she considered Jason's proposal. You're so soft-hearted, aren't you, despite all that's happened to you?' She reached into a pocket for her knife. 'But it's not going to get you anywhere. Some people are just bad and there's nothing anyone can do to help.'

Jason gulped as Lori flipped out a long, slender blade and pointed it at his chest before slowly moving it upwards and stopping at his throat. 'So if this is the only way I can prove to you that I'm right, then so be it.' She lowered the knife and climbed into the back seat. She cut through the ropes mercilessly until his wrists were free and he was no longer imprisoned in his seat.

'There you are… free at last!' said Lori with regret in her voice as she put away her knife and leant back against the seat. Jason rubbed at his wrists where the ropes had left their mark, until the numbness had left his fingers, and winced in discomfort as the blood began to circulate again through his hands and arms.

He froze as he heard the hammer being pulled back on Lori's gun. 'Put that away will you. I told you I can handle this myself.' Jason didn't dare move.

'Relax, just making sure I'm ready in case your little plan falls apart,' said Lori.

'It won't, they're just kids, I can do this,' said Jason, acting as if he was trying to convince himself more than Lori. 'I just need you to stay in here while I talk to them. Can you do that for me?'

At that moment he caught sight of a young girl coming out of the flats. 'Is that the one?' he asked, not taking his eyes off her.

'Looks like it.' Lori watched from her window as the girl walked past the car and headed in the direction of the playground where the gang of bullies was waiting for her.

'What an ugly child… no wonder she's getting bullied,' she sniggered leaning forward to keep a close eye on the girl. Jason's disgust at her remarks was evident. 'Will you lighten up! I'm just having a laugh.'

Jason waited until the girl was only a few yards from the playground, but before he could reach for the door handle to make his move Lori grabbed his arm to stop him from getting out. 'Let's see what happens first before you go marching over there. Don't forget some of the entries written in the book aren't always correct. Let's just make sure there are no mistakes.' Jason remained in his seat as they both waited to see what would happen next.

The gang of bullies, consisting of three girls and one wimpy-looking boy, quickly circled the girl who somehow managed to keep a brave face pinned on despite being subjected to a barrage of insults.

'All right, lard arse, you took your time... Come on then, hand it over,' said the hard-faced ringleader, who was really in no position to be making insults about anyone's weight.

'I... I haven't got it... well, at least not all of it,' said the girl, her soft voice trembling and her hand shaking uncontrollably as she reached into her pocket and pulled out two tatty twenty pound notes. 'I could only manage to scrape together forty but I can get you the other sixty by tomorrow afternoon.'

'That's not good enough,' spat the ringleader, not accepting the money being offered. 'You said you'd have it all by tonight... you gave us your word.'

'I know, but my aunt didn't turn up today... she rang earlier saying she'd be over tomorrow instead... so as soon as she gives me my money for Christmas I'll meet you back here to pay the rest.'

'Bullshit!' interrupted the boy with a tough voice that didn't match his wimpy appearance. 'What if her aunt doesn't turn up tomorrow? She'll have us waiting out here in the cold again for nothing.'

'He's got a point, Kim,' said one of the other girls standing next to him. 'How can we be sure she's not just fobbing us off?'

Kim pushed a stray strand of her red hair behind her ear and looked as if she was ready to pounce on the girl at any minute.

'I reckon we should teach the fat bitch a lesson for messing us around,' added her friend, pushing the girl from behind.

'No, please. I promise I'll pay you the rest tomorrow... I swear on my Nan's grave,' said the girl, her watery eyes gleaming behind her glasses as the bullies moved closer to her like a pack of wolves around a frightened deer.

'Tell you what... we'll take this forty off you as compensation,' said Kim, snatching the money out of the girl's hand. 'But we still want a hundred off you tomorrow. '

'But how am I supposed to get that? I'm only getting fifty off my aunt tomorrow. I was going to sell my 3DS to raise the other ten... and you know my parents are skint.'

'Well, that's not my problem is it, love?' Kim smirked. You're just going to have to find a way to make the extra forty, because if you come here tomorrow without it... not only will I expose you for the big fat slag you are, but I promise you'll be re-united with your Nan sooner then you think.' She grabbed the girl by her hair and pulled her head back, before shoving her hard onto the ground.

'That's enough... leaver her alone!' shouted Jason, almost slipping on the icy grass as he stepped off the pavement and hurried towards the playground where the girl was being attacked by the bullies with kicks and punches. 'Get away from her,' he demanded, pushing through the group of teenagers.

'This doesn't concern you, Mr, stay out of it!' said Kim, fuming over Jason's interference.

'Are there enough of you to cope with one girl?' asked Jason, helping the girl to her feet and keeping her close to him.

'What are you, her sugar daddy?' asked Kim, eliciting loud laughter from her friends.

'He's a bit old for you isn't he, love?' added the boy

'No. I'm a police community support officer, and if you don't leave this girl alone you're all going to be in deep trouble.' Jason's heavy breathing misted the air in front of his face.

'You don't look like a pig to me,' said Kim, folding her arms, unconvinced. 'If I didn't know any better I'd say this little tramp 'as put you up to this to try and scare us off.'

'I haven't... I swear I've never seen him before in my life,' the girl sobbed.

'Now, I'm serious... if I catch any of you hassling this girl again I'll...'

'You'll what, old man?' Kim asked, cutting Jason off. 'Do what you like, you ain't scaring no one, pal... because I promise, whatever happens to us, that fat tramp will be the one who ends up paying for it. In fact, because of your interference the debt as just gone up; after you pay us tomorrow we want another hundred off you next week or else!'

'You're not getting another penny out of her, tomorrow or next week,' said Jason. 'Now, I know where you all live, so I warn you, if I hear of any of you bothering this girl again not only will I have a word with your parents, I'll see to it that each of you spends the next three years in a youth offenders' institute.'

'Man, who do you think you are?' said Kim. 'There's four of us... you're hardly in any position to be dishing out orders.'

At this, Jason became alarmed and held the girl closer as the group of teenagers began to circle them both looking as if they were planning to give him the same treatment.

'I'd do what he says if I were you, carrot top, or you might just live to regret it... and believe me when I say might.' Jason breathed a sigh of relief at the sight of Lori standing next to him.

'Blimey, not another one!' said Kim, sniggering at Lori. 'First it's him, now it's some hooker. Bit nippy for your line of work ain't it, love? It must get real cold hanging about the streets at this time of year.'

'Not half as cold as you're gonna be if you don't hop it,' said Lori getting right in the ringleader's face.

Kim backed up a few steps having seen the crazy look in Lori's eyes daring her to make one wrong move. 'Lucky I've got to be somewhere else in a bit,' she said, dropping her gaze and backing further away.

'Oh, trust me, you have no idea how lucky you are,' said Lori.

Kim gave the girl a look that could kill before beating a hasty retreat. 'Come on, guys, let's get outta here.'

'This ain't over, you fat tramp,' the boy warned as he and other two girls followed their leader out of the playground.

Jason waited until the gang were out of sight before returning his attention to the girl. 'It's okay now, they've gone, you don't have to be scared any more,' he said, gently putting a hand on her shoulder.

'No... why did you have to interfere,' said the girl. 'You've made things ten times worse for me now.'

'Hey... it's okay,' said Jason, trying to comfort her.

'It's not okay... it'll never be okay thanks to you.' The girl pushed him away. 'You should've just left me alone. Why can't everyone just leave me alone?'

Jason was lost for words as the girl ran back towards the flats sobbing as she went.

'Nice going, Jason, you really screwed that one up,' said Lori, giving him a slow hand clap.

'What are you talking about? I saved her didn't I?'

'Only time will tell.'

'I proved you wrong; there is another way of doing this without anyone having to get killed.'

'Don't get ahead of yourself, the night isn't over yet,' said Lori, laughing at Jason's sureness.

'Well, it is for me, because I've made up my mind and I've decided that I don't want to join you. This ends here.'

'This ends when I say it ends, is that understood,' said Lori, pointing her gun at Jason. 'Now, I've got some good news and some bad news for you, Mr. The good news is, if that's your decision then I will respect it, so you won't be coming with me on my next trip. The bad news, however, is that I'm not scheduled to set off until tomorrow morning so we won't be saying our goodbyes just yet.'

'So what are we going to do for the rest of the night?'

'There's a hotel about two miles down the road from here; we'll stay there for the night.'

'Then what?'

'Then I'm going to have a long hot bath and get a good nights sleep,' said Lori, relishing the thought.

'That's not what I was asking.'

'Oh, you mean then what for you? erm... well, let me see...' Lori was thinking to herself as she lowered her gun. 'If you can behave yourself for the rest of the night you'll be free to go in the morning.'

'What... you're just going to let me go?' Lori shrugged her shoulders and nodded.

'But aren't you afraid I'll go to the police and tell them all that I've witnessed?'

'Oh, yeah, really afraid. I can just see their faces now when you tell them that a young woman with information from the future kidnapped you and took you across the country on a killing spree!'

'I know your name... I may even memorise the registration of your car,' Jason reminded her.

'No, Jason, you only know the name I told you; that doesn't necessarily mean it's my real name. Oh, and by the way, I don't think it would be a good idea for you to memorise the car's number plate, especially as it's registered in your name!'

'What?' said Jason, looking back to where the car was parked.

'Don't look so shocked. I did tell you I've been planning this for quite some time. And it was so easy to forge your signature.' Lori folded her arms trying to keep warm in the cold night air and smiled.

'Don't believe me? Maybe when you get home you can have a little look through that big stack of unopened letters in your hallway – I'm sure you'll find the log book in there somewhere. Even if you do go to the police how do you know they won't think you went on some kind of drunken bender and did all those killings yourself. I bet the press would eat that story up… ex-PCSO turned alcoholic, turns psycho! They could turn it all into a movie in years to come… you might even get a few crappy sequels too, if you're lucky.'

Jason was indignant. 'You're enjoying this, aren't you?'

'I beg your pardon?' said Lori with a bemused expression.

'Setting me up like this… you evil, twisted…'

'Careful, Jason, I'm just covering my tracks. As long as you keep your mouth shut we'll both have nothing to worry about. Here, I've done enough driving for one day; you can take us to the hotel.'

Lori threw Jason the keys before heading back to the car. 'Well, are you coming or not? You haven't forgotten how to drive have you?' She glanced back at Jason who was a little reluctant to follow. He was standing on the spot staring down at the keys in his hand, contemplating whether or not he should toss them into some nearby bushes and make a quick run for it while there was still enough distance between him and Lori. But the ground was covered in frost and patches of snow and he realised that, even if he were lucky enough to out-run her on the slippery surface, there was certainly no chance of out-running one of her bullets. So, with no other choice he headed in her direction.

'Hurry up and unlock this thing will you, it's bloody freezing out here.' Lori looked every bit the she devil as she leant against the car with arms folded waiting for him to catch up.

Jason pressed the button on the key fob to unlock the doors and seemed a little uneasy when Lori opened the driver's rear passenger side.

'You're riding in the back?' he asked nervously. How can I be sure you're not planning to shoot me in the back of the head while I'm driving?'

Lori rolled her eyes heavenwards. 'Jason, trust me, if I was going to shoot you I would've already done it by now. I've told you I would never hurt you unless you were to try something stupid, which is the reason why I'm riding in the back. Now, can we please get in the car before I get frostbite?'

Jason got in despite his misgivings and soon found himself taking directions from Lori to get to the hotel.

Whatever was to happen to him that night, whether or not Lori would stay true to her word and let him go the very next morning, or if he was never to see the light of day again, at least he could take comfort in knowing that he had saved a young girl's life while preventing her bullies from meeting a sticky end at the hands of the Assassin.

CHAPTER 9 - WHAT WILL BE WILL BE

Jason had been staring up at the cracked ceiling of the shabby hotel room for what seemed like hours still struggling to come to terms with the horrible events of the past day. Both his hands were cuffed to the wooden bed frame where he lay uncomfortably on a lumpy mattress. Every attempt at sleep had been interrupted by Lori singing 'Que sera, sera, Whatever will be, will be' from the bathroom in a ridiculously loud voice as if she had just come home from a normal day at work and was getting ready for bed.

'This isn't fair you know... I gave you my word... I told you I'm not going to try anything,' he called out to her. 'It's not like I'm the dangerous one in this room.' He lifted his head from the flat pillow in frustration and watched Lori's shadow dancing in the light that spilled under the bathroom door. He could hear the gurgling sound of water draining out of the bath and before he could say another word the door swung open revealing a cloud of steam from which Lori appeared with a purple towel wrapped around her body and another around her head, turban style.

'Sorry, what was that?' she said, humming the rest of the song and grabbing her toilet bag from a shelf under the television.

Jason waited until she'd settled herself down on the edge of the bed before speaking. 'I was saying why must I be a prisoner again? You know I'm not going to try anything especially now that we're so close to the end.'

'Oh, stop your whining will you,' said Lori, going through her usual routine of patting herself dry before applying moisturiser to her face and body. 'I'm just making sure you don't get any funny ideas while I'm sleeping. Now, just relax and it'll be morning before you know it.'

'Yeah? Well it can't come a moment too soon,' said Jason, taking a keen interest in the tattoo on Lori's right arm which as far as he could tell appeared to be some sort of flag showing a red wagon wheel at the centre of a blue and green background and bearing the words 'Romani' at the top and 'Pen' at the bottom.

'You say that now, but I bet as soon as you step back inside that empty little house of yours you'll be wishing you were right back here next to me.' Lori applied the last of the moisturiser to her legs and lay down next to Jason. 'Aww, that feels so much better. I'm going to sleep like a log tonight. Something on your mind, Jase?' she asked, with a little yawn.

'Don't you feel any kind of remorse for what you've done today?'

'Well, not really... they chose their own fate. Why should I lose any sleep when all I've done is saved a few people's lives from an arsonist, a paedophile and a reckless drunk driver? I probably would've lost more sleep if I hadn't stopped them,' said Lori with a smile. 'It's a shame you can't see the bigger picture... but I guess I'll just have to find someone who will.'

'What? You're going to put someone else through the same torture as me?'

'Well, I don't have much choice now that you've turned me down.' A tiny flush of pleasure appeared in Lori's cheeks and a cruel smile began to curl her lips. 'Are you sure that's what you really want though?' Her gaze met Jason's once more as she turned on her side and ran her fingers lightly across his face. 'It's such a shame we have to go our separate ways tomorrow when there's so much chemistry between us.'

Jason found himself blushing. 'Chemistry?'

'Don't deny it; I know you've felt it too.' She moved so close to him that she could feel his heart beating.

'After what you've put me through in the last twenty-four hours, believe me I feel nothing for you but contempt,' said Jason, trying hard to fight the impulses coursing through his body.

'You've had plenty of opportunities to escape if you'd really wanted to, yet here you are, still happy to play my little prisoner.'

Jason swallowed hard as Lori moved her fingers slowly from his face to his chest. 'You forced me into that taxi... all I wanted to do was go home.'

'You got into that taxi of your own free will. All I did was offer you a lift and, you know what, I don't think you regret it.' Lori's fingers moved down his chest towards his belt. 'In fact I'm betting that way down inside you don't want to leave me any more than I want to leave you.'

Jason was unable to deny that every word Lori spoke was true. 'I've seen the way you look at me,' she said. 'Just admit it... you're crazy about me. You long to tame that wild side of me; I can see it in your eyes.' She removed the towel from her head allowing her damp hair to fall around her shoulders.

'I don't think you could ever be tamed.' Jason's voice was barely a whisper.

'Maybe you're right, but I guess it can't hurt to try.'

Lori tilted her head up for a kiss, but somehow Jason found the strength to turn his face away, leaving her to smile in disappointment. 'If you think that seducing me is going to persuade me to join you, you're very much mistaken.'

'Aww, Jase, I wasn't trying to seduce you. I just thought I could get something out of this whole thing so that it wouldn't turn out to be a complete waste of time.' She playfully hit him over the head with a pillow before getting up and grabbing the car keys from the bedside table. 'I've just remembered I've left the book on the back seat of the car.' Grabbing his coat to cover herself, she headed for the door. 'This is a rough area, someone might break in. The last thing we want is for it to fall into the wrong hands.'

'I think it's a bit late for that!'

If Lori heard Jason's remark before she left the room she didn't let it show and by the time she returned he was sound asleep.

*

Next morning after a long, uncomfortable night, drifting in and out of sleep, Jason awoke from yet another nightmare. Only this time it wasn't the faces of his ex-wife and daughter who haunted his dreams, but the tragic souls of Lori's victims. Two of them had been standing at either side of his bed, one with a gun shot wound in his head, the other with a knife sticking out of his rib cage, while a third stood at the foot of the bed with icicles dripping from his ears, nose and chin. He stared at Jason with a blank expression before joining his companions as they had let out a mournful cry of anguish, stretching out their arms as if pleading for Jason to help them find some sort of retribution for Lori's actions.

Jason sat up in bed trying to shake of the ghostly voices still ringing in his head from the nightmare, only realising that his hands were free when he was forced to shield his eyes from the bright morning sun as Lori walked over to the window and drew back the curtains.

'It's about time you were up,' she said, pushing the window open so she could light up a cigarette despite the rush of cold air chilling her to the bone.

'What time is it?' Jason asked, relieved that Lori had kept her word and he was still in one piece.

'It's gone half ten... I've been up for hours.' She was fully dressed in dark blue jeans and a black top. 'I did try waking you but you were out cold.'

'Yeah, well you'll have to excuse me if I overslept, I didn't exactly get a good nights rest,' he grumbled.

'Aww, never mind, at least you didn't get to witness one of my hair brushing tantrums.' Lori exhaled a little cloud of smoke out of the window. 'After I finish this fag I'll make us a nice cup of coffee.'

'Aren't you supposed to be somewhere else by now,' said Jason, sitting on the side of the bed and rubbing his aching wrists.

'Well, I wasn't about to leave without saying goodbye to you first,' said Lori, raising an eyebrow.

'Let me save you the trouble... goodbye!' Jason slipped on his shoes and coat before heading for the door.

'Wait... don't go!' Lori tossed what was left of her cigarette out of the window. 'Please stay with me a little bit longer.' She linked her arm through his and led him to the foot of the bed so they could both sit down.

'I thought you said I'd be free to go.' He realised that saying goodbye to Lori was definitely the right thing to do even if it wasn't what he really wanted.

'You are free to go, but let's just spend a bit more time together before we go our separate ways,' she said in a small, sad voice.

'There's no point.' Jason put his arm around her as she grasped his other hand in both of hers. 'You have to let me go,' he said softly.

'I know, I just can't bear to watch you walk out of my life for ever.' Lori rested her head against his chest. 'I wish there was a way I could make you stay, but I know there isn't,' she said, while keeping a close eye on the morning news airing on the television in front of the bed with the volume turned down low. 'The worst part for me is knowing that you're probably going to walk away today hating me for everything I've put you through.'

Jason was moved by the regret in Lori's voice and for a moment found it difficult to find the right words of comfort. 'That's not true.' He gently rested his chin on the top of her head. 'I guess I should hate you, but I don't. Despite everything you've made me feel like I'm needed again and I'm grateful to you for that.'

Lori lifted and head and smiled, enjoying being close to him. As she leant forward intending to kiss him his attention was diverted to the TV as a familiar face appeared on the screen.

'Lori, look... it's the girl from last night.' He got off the bed and rushed over to the set to turn up the volume.

'What… Jase what on earth are you talking about?' said Lori, playing dumb while he stood in stunned silence looking at the picture of the young girl who he thought he'd rescued from the gang of bullies the night before.

'It can't be true,' he said listening in shock as the news reporter explained that a sixteen-year old girl had been found hanged in her bedroom in the early hours of the morning, after a humiliating video of her was posted on line.

'Oh, you mean that girl.'

Lori got off the bed and stood next to Jason who looked at her in total confusion. 'She… she committed suicide? But I thought you said her death would be caused by the bullies.'

'And it was. They blackmailed her until she reached the point where she felt she had no other choice but to do the unthinkable.' Lori's voice was firm but tender.

'But you said they assaulted her,' said Jason, trying to make sense of it all.

'Sometimes a verbal assault can be just as harmful as a physical one,' replied Lori with a heavy sigh.

'That poor girl.' Jason turned back to the television.

'Don't blame yourself, Jase; you did your best for her.' Lori softly touched his shoulder to reassure him.

'A lot of good it did her. I probably made things ten times worse for the poor kid.' His eyes filled with tears as one final image of the girl was shown before the news reader moved on to the rest of the day's stories.

Lori switched off the TV, put her hand on Jason's cheek and turned his face towards her. 'Listen to me, nothing you could've said or done would've stopped those kids from posting that video on line. Even if you were to offer them all the money in the world, they still would've done it.'

'But maybe I went about it the wrong way... maybe if I'd tried another way they might've ...'

Jason wanted to say more but Lori pressed her finger against his lips. 'Ssh... there is no other way, Jase, believe me. The only way that girl would've lived was if her bullies had died. Surely even you can now see that? If we'd only done things my way that poor girl would still be alive.'

'And four others would be dead!' retorted Jason.

'Better to let four bad people die so that one good person can live, wouldn't you agree?' Lori's gaze was unwavering.

'I don't know... I just don't know anymore.'

'Well, you're gonna have to decide because we've reached the crossroads. I've shown you all I can and I've said all I can say. It's up to you now to make up your mind which road you want to take. Do you go back home and hide yourself away from the world and do nothing while good people like your family and mine are being killed needlessly. Or do you come with me and make sure that no one ever has to go through the pain that we both have... the same pain that, no doubt, that poor girl's family will be going through today?'

'Lori... I can't kill people.'

'I know that and I'm not asking you to. All I want is to have someone like you by my side, to have my back and be there for me. We could be there for each other. That's all I'm asking of you... I'll do the rest.' Jason closed his eyes not knowing how to answer.

'Look, I really should be getting a move one,' she said, glancing at her watch. 'I wish I could stay here until you've made up your mind but I haven't got time... so here, I want you to take this.' She handed Jason a folded piece of paper. 'It's the time and location of where I'll be tonight... I wrote it down earlier. It's not all that far from where you live, so go home and have a good long think about what you want to do. If you decide that you'd like to join me, then you'll know where I'll be.'

Lori planted a kiss on his forehead before grabbing her bag from under the bed, her leather jacket from the back of a chair and making her way to the door. 'I'm not really one for saying goodbyes so I'll just say see you later.' She opened the door.

'Wait!' Jason called. 'How am I supposed to get home? I don't even know where I am.'

Lori smiled. 'There's a station about a mile down the road. I put a hundred quid inside your coat pocket this morning. That should be more than enough to buy you a nice breakfast and a train ticket home.'

Jason wiped his eyes and gave her a grateful smile. 'Well, have a safe journey home and I hope to see you soon,' said Lori, pulling the door closed behind her and leaving him alone with just his thoughts.

He unfolded the piece of paper in his hand and stared at Lori's clumsy handwriting – 'BE AT NUMBER 28 ASH GROVE IN DARWEN, LANCASHIRE BEFORE 9pm TONIGHT. NO LATER! LOTS OF LOVE, LORI XXX.' Then refolding the note he pushed it into his coat pocket and walked over to the window. Her car was parked in front of the hotel and he watched as she unlocked the door and hurriedly threw her coat and bag onto the back seat, stopping only once to de-ice the windows. She turned to wave goodbye and blow him a kiss before jumping into the driving seat and speeding off down the road to her next destination.

Jason let out a sigh of relief as the car disappeared from view and leant his back against the wall unsure whether he was happy or sad to see her go. He stood there lost in thought until the cleaners came to do the room reminding him that the time had come for him to make the long journey home.

*

Later that day after managing some breakfast, Jason sat on a train bound for home, watching as fields and villages flew past his window like a speeded up movie, and listening to two elderly ladies in the seats behind him who were chatting about the day's gossip.

'So I said to her, be thankful for what you've got. In my day we'd think ourselves lucky if we had food on the table at Christmas, let alone silly presents,' said one.

'She should be grateful she's got a nice husband and three lovely children,' said the other.'

'She should indeed, especially with all the terrible things that's going on in the world... did you hear about that poor young girl from Bristol?'

'Wasn't it awful? I can't imagine how her parents must be feeling; I hope they find the little sods who were the cause of it.'

Jason closed his eyes and tried to block out the sound of their voices. Even though he knew the girl's death had nothing to do with him, still he couldn't help but feel partly responsible for what had happened to her.

Arriving at his destination he moved away from the hustle and bustle of the station and shortly found himself standing in the eerie silence and freezing cold of the cemetery at the graveside of his beloved ex-wife and daughter.

'Sorry it's taken me so long to come,' he said, as he wiped the snow away from their pictures attached to the marble headstone. 'I just couldn't find the strength to face up to it. I want you to know that there isn't a moment that goes by when I don't think about you both, and I'd do anything right now to have you here with me… if only for a moment.'

Jason wiped his eyes and smiled at Jessica's picture. 'I don't know what I should do. I don't know what's right or wrong any more. I promise I'll come to see you again very soon. Sleep peacefully, my angels.' He carefully placed a beautiful bunch of flowers in front of the gravestone before turning and making for the gate.

It was dark when he arrived home and, as Lori had warned him, he began to wish that he had never returned to his cold and lonely house. He switched on the lights as he passed through the hall, angrily throwing off his coat as he entered the living room. He'd only been away for two nights but it felt more like a lifetime and the very thought of sitting all by himself again and slipping back into his old habits was enough to make him want to leave the house and never return.

'Do you go home and do nothing while good people like your family and mine are being killed needlessly, or do you come with me and together we can make sure that no one has to go through the same pain that we have, ever again?' Lori's words kept coming back to him as he paced up and down trying to reach a decision.

Then he noticed the red light on the answerphone blinking and pressed play to discover who had left him a message.

'Hello, Jase, it's Rachel... I'm just calling to remind you that the Christmas Eve mass starts at six thirty in the Cathedral. I hope you're still coming because I've promised my boys that you'll be there. I hope you don't mind but it's the only way I could get them to take part in the children's choir. The other thing is that your parents can't come because your father's not up to it, but they send their love and would like you to pay them a visit if you can before the New Year. I'll save you a seat next to me and Gary in the top right-hand pew. See you soon... bye.'

'Oh crap!' Jason ran his fingers through his hair in frustration when the recording ended. Everything that had happened to him in the last forty-eight hours had made him completely forget his promise to Rachel and, even though church was probably the last place on earth he wanted to be at that point, he couldn't let her down, especially after all she'd done for him over the past year.

Next minute he was running upstairs to the bathroom to get washed and ready to go and meet her and her family at the Cathedral.

CHAPTER 10 - FAITH AND FRIENDSHIP

St John's Cathedral stood at the heart of Salford surrounded by neatly trimmed trees, hedges and lawns. It had elegant stained-glass windows and a central tower and spire rising above the roof of the neo-Gothic style building.

Jason could hear the faint sound of organ music playing as he walked through the grounds and headed towards the main entrance where he was met by a wall of warmth as he stepped inside and slowly made his way to the front of the pews. Heads turned and sly nudges were exchanged by members of the congregation who were more than a little surprised to see the man who they believed to be dead to the world joining them for Christmas Eve mass.

But he kept his eyes to the ground, ignoring the whispers and shocked faces, until he came to where his friends were seated. Rachel leapt up at once and greeted him with a huge hug, overjoyed that not only had he kept his promise to her but that he was looking more like his old self again, clean shaven and dressed in a suit. Her husband Gary welcomed him with a handshake before making room for Jason to join them in their pew.

A bell rang and the congregation stood as a group of young children dressed as shepherds, angels and the three Wise Men, followed the priest towards the altar where they stood quietly while he performed the usual rituals of making the sign of the cross and reading a few introductory prayers. He gave a brief explanation of the Nativity before the children sang their first hymn of the night, 'A beautiful angel came to a hill'.

At first, Jason felt a little uncomfortable to be sitting in such a place after everything he'd witnessed in the past twenty-four hours, but as soon as the children started to sing he began to feel more settled and at ease, even finding himself smiling at one point as he glanced at the proud mother next to him weeping tears of joy at the sight of her two little shepherds singing their hearts out.

When he looked back at the children something wonderful happened. Whether his eyes were playing tricks or whether he was just imagining it, he was almost certain he could see the smiling face of his own little girl, dressed as an angel and singing with the rest of the group, as if she were giving him a sign not to be sad anymore but to be happy knowing that she was with her mother in a much better place where they would all meet again one day. And by the time the hymn was over Jason, too, had tears in his eyes.

The rest of the mass was beautiful; more hymns and carols were sung by the children while more prayers and lessons were read by the priest and members of the congregation. Jason was so caught up in the atmosphere that he found himself wishing the service would never end.

But the clock was ticking and he realised that he would soon need to make a move if he was going to take up the offer made to him by Lori. As Rachel and her husband left their seats to join the queue to receive Holy Communion Jason took the perfect opportunity to tip toe down the side aisle and make for the exit. The wooden Cathedral doors made a loud creaking sound as he pushed them open and let them swing to behind him. His breath clouded in the frosty air as he let out a sigh of relief believing that no one had noticed him slipping away.

It wasn't until he was half way along the flagstone path through the grounds that he was stopped in his tracks by the sound of Rachel's voice calling him. 'Jase, were you going to leave without saying goodbye?' She looked like an angel herself with her hair blowing in the breeze as she made her way towards him along the path that glistened in the half light of the moon on the snow.

'Sorry, I was just trying to avoid the crowds,' said Jason, feeling a little embarrassed.

'I had a feeling you might.'

He shrugged his shoulders. 'I guess you know me too well.'

Rachel laughed and brushed a stray strand of hair off her face. 'Well, thanks for coming tonight. I can't tell you how much it meant to me to have you here and to see you looking like your old self again.'

'It's the least I could do after everything you've done for me over the past year. Rach listen, I'm glad you're here now because I might be going away for a little while and I was going to leave you a letter asking if you would be kind enough to keep an eye on the house for me while I'm gone.'

'You're going away? Where are you going to?' Rachel seemed rather taken aback.

'I don't know for sure yet and I don't know for how long... I just hope you can understand.' His expression gave no suggestion of what was on his mind.

'I understand.' Rachel smiled without further question. 'You do whatever is best for you. I won't stand in your way and don't worry about the house... I'll keep a close eye on it for you until you're ready to come back. So, is there anything else you want to tell me before you leave or should I just read the letter?' she smiled, her eyes shining with humour.

Jason laughed and his expression dispelled the twinge of concern she had felt. 'Actually there is... I just want to say thank you. You've been an angel... I know you said it's good to have me here tonight, but the truth is, if it wasn't for you I probably wouldn't be standing here at all. You've helped me through a lot of tough times and you never once gave up on me even when I gave you every reason to walk away. I won't forget what you've done for me... not ever.'

'Think nothing of it. I know you would've done the same for me, and I was just remembering something you said once.'

'What did I say?' Jason looked confused.

'You said that the true heroes of this world are the ones that make a difference to people's lives by a kind act or a kind word when it's needed most. Now it's a good thing I chased after you because otherwise I wouldn't have been able to give you your present.' Rachel handed Jason a parcel neatly wrapped in Christmas paper.

'You shouldn't have bothered,' he said, graciously taking the gift that was being handed to him.

'We wanted to... it's from all of us. Maybe you can open it after I'm gone,' she suggested.

Jason expected her to leave there and then, but instead she continued to stand in front of him as if there was more she needed to share before they could say goodbye. 'Listen, there's something else I want you to have before you go.'

She reached to the back of her neck to remove the thin gold chain she wore. 'I keep this with me everywhere I go. It's the necklace you gave me after my mother died.' She wrapped the chain around her fingers and held the small round pendant in the palm of her hand. 'I was fourteen years old and you were about to leave for college, but the day before you left you gave me this and said if ever there was a time when I should feel down or troubled, all I had to do was to read the short prayer on the pendant and it would give me strength. And you were right, it did, and I believe it even helped me to find my true vocation in life. So, now that you're leaving me again, I want you to take it back and do the same.'

'No, Rach, I can't take it… it was a gift to you.'

'Just take it, please,' she insisted. 'And when you find your true vocation in life, whatever it may be, then you can give it back to me.'

Jason smiled at her as he took the pendant from her hand. 'Just remember to believe in yourself and believe in others,' she said.

Snow began to fall gently as they shared a farewell hug. Then they heard Gary calling to her from the steps of the Cathedral, and she kissed Jason on the cheek before turning to go.

Gary exchanged a friendly wave with Jason as he waited for his wife to join him, and before they disappeared through the doors Rachel turned and gave Jason an encouraging smile.

He looked down at the pendant seeing the design of the praying hands on one side and turning it over to the prayer engraved on the other side which read, 'God grant me the serenity to accept the things I cannot change, the courage to change the things I can, and the wisdom to know the difference.'

He clutched it tightly in his hand and felt his spirits lift. Then he turned to his present and when he'd unwrapped the paper was astonished and pleased to see his photo and his medal for bravery that he'd tried to destroy only a few days before. Now they sat in a brand new silver frame capturing all that he was and all that he could be again if only he gave his mind to it.

And by the time the mass ended and the congregation began to depart, Jason was already on his way to the appointed meeting with Lori.

CHAPTER 11 - THE KNIGHT BEFORE CHRISTMAS

It was ten past nine when Lori finally accepted that Jason wasn't coming to meet her, and it was only then that she realised how much she had been looking forward to seeing him.

Snow crunched under her feet as she sneaked her way around the side of a shabby terraced house, careful not to knock over any rubbish bins or anything else that might raise the alarm and alert the neighbours. At the back door she had to forcefully shoo a cranky cat away from the kitchen window with a handful of snow so that she could see what was going on inside. Voices were raised in heated argument and through a gap in the curtains she could clearly see a pregnant woman being pushed around the kitchen by the man she knew to be the husband. As the shouting grew louder and the violence began to escalate Lori calmly pulled up the hood of her cloak and freed her gun.

'Please, Josh, you're hurting me,' said the woman as her husband pushed her against the worktop and grabbed her by the hair to tilt her face up. 'I swear to you I'm not going anywhere.'

The man's face twisted into an ugly smile and he looked down at her, his skin dripping with perspiration and his eyes filled with rage. 'Then why would your sister send you those text messages?'

'What messages?' said the woman letting out a wail of pain as he pulled her hair harder and held a mobile phone to her face.

'Don't play dumb with me, you lying bitch!' he spat. 'It's all on here... "You have to leave him Tania, he's no good for you babe, next time he loses his temper he could hurt you and the baby, you can stay with me until you sort out a place to live, you'll be safe here I promise"' he read before throwing the phone hard onto the floor. 'Well? What have you got to say about that?'

'She's just worried about me, that's all, now please let go of me,' said the sobbing woman.

The man moved his other hand to her throat and squeezed. 'I knew it was a mistake to let you visit her... she's always trying to poison your mind against me, the evil jealous...'

His tirade was interrupted as his wife managed to grab a plate from the worktop and smash it over his head before making a dash for the front door. But his hand snaked out to wrench her back and in the struggle they both fell to the floor.

'You're not going anywhere, do you hear me? YOU'RE NOT GOING ANYWHERE!' he said, gaining control by wrapping an arm around her neck making it difficult for her to breathe.

The woman tried to free herself but he easily thwarted her attempts to escape and her struggles only made her lose air faster. On the verge of passing out, she stopped fighting. Her husband released his hold and staggered to his feet in terror as the kitchen door burst open and in walked a hooded figure pointing a gun straight at him.

The man raised both hands and slowly backed out of the kitchen with Lori following him looking like the grim reaper with her hood covering most of her face.

At the door of the living room he began to plead for his life. 'Wait, don't shoot... you don't understand. I wasn't going to hurt her... things just got out of hand... You don't have to do this, please give me another chance.' He continued to back away from the Assassin, almost knocking over a chair in the process.

A wicked smile appeared on Lori's face as she cornered him in the hallway and, relishing the moment, pulled back the hammer on the gun. 'People like you don't deserve another chance.'

The man flinched and covered his face with his arms as Lori pulled the trigger. To her horror the gun didn't fire. She pulled again and still nothing.

'Oh, shit!' she said after the pistol failed her for the third time and the man ducked as she threw her weapon directly at him and made a run for it back to the kitchen door.

He grabbed her by the hood of her cloak and yanked her towards him before throwing her hard onto the floor. 'Come into my house to try and kill me, would you?' he said, trying to keep Lori down with his full body weight on top of her.

His wife screamed in fright, got to her feet and made a speedy exit, not once looking back.

'Let go of me, you big dosser!' said Lori, struggling to free herself from the man's clutches, the man secured his hold.

'Sorry, but you've entered the wrong house today, you psychotic bitch,' he said, spraying her with spit.

'That's right... I got the wrong house... I was meant to go next door to number 27. Now, let me go!' She thrust with her hips to buck him off only to have her attempt met with a laugh as the man placed his hands around her neck and applied pressure.

Lori tried to turn her head to break his hold and with her free hand attempted to reach into a pocket for her knife, but his grip was much too strong. Her face reddened and her eyes watered as her vision became blurred. Then relief... she felt the hands loosen, cool air rushed into her lungs and she breathed deeply and gratefully as she regained her senses.

'Are you ok?' said Jason, throwing down the frying pan that he'd used to strike the man and helping Lori to her feet.

'Oh, Jase, I knew you'd come,' she said cheerfully throwing her arms around him. 'I thought I was a goner then for sure. Thank you for rescuing me, my knight in shining armour.'

'Are you sure you're alright?' he said gently.

'I am now,' Lori smiled at him before turning her attention to the man on the floor who was trying to crawl away. 'Right then, let's give bully boy a taste of his own medicine, shall we?'

She ripped a phone charger from the wall socket and wrapped it around the man's throat. 'How do you like it, hey? Not very nice is it?' Thirsty for revenge and enjoying every sound coming from the man fighting for air, she pressed her knee against his back to tighten her grip even more.

But Jason intervened and Lori was still aiming kicks at the man as he pulled her into the hallway.

'Jason let go of me, I'm not finished with him yet.' About to take another charge at the man lying helplessly on the floor, Lori felt the cold metal of handcuffs clamp her wrist to the bannisters. 'What are you doing?'

He took a few steps back to the living room. 'I'm sorry, Lori, this has to end here.'

'You can't be serious?' she said in disbelief, trying to wrench her arm free. 'Jase, you can't do this… we have work to do, these people have to be stopped… you know that!'

'I've made my decision and I'll be taking over from here. I will stop these people but I won't kill them. Things are going to be done differently from now on, without anyone having to die.'

A look of horror clouded Lori's face as she sat uselessly on the floor. 'So that's why you're here? You're going to turn me in?' she said.

He came closer and squatted in front of her. 'I've already called the police; they'll be here any minute.'

'Don't suppose you know a good solicitor? They're gonna throw away the key once they catch me.'

'Believe me, I don't want to do this, Lori, but...'

'But you have no choice,' she interrupted. 'It's okay, I understand, I knew this would happen eventually. I was either gonna get caught or get killed. That's the whole reason I wanted you to join me, so you could prevent the inevitable.'

'Don't think I'm doing this out of hate, Lori, in fact, I care about you and I forgive you for everything you've done. I know that whatever happened to you in the past has made you lose your way, and somewhere inside, under all that grief, there's still a good person crying out to be found.'

Lori tried to hold back her tears as police sirens sounded in the distance. 'You don't have to worry... I won't ever tell anyone we know each other... now you'd best get going if you don't want the police to think you had any part in all this.'

With a sad smile Lori reached into her pocket for the car keys. 'Take these... the book is on the back seat along with a few of my belongings.'

Jason took the keys from her hand and straightened up. 'I wish there was another way,' he said softly.

'There is no other way, Jason... you've made up your mind. Now just get going before the police get here.'

Jason fiddled with the car keys as if there was more he wanted to say if only he could find the right words.

As he turned to leave Lori called him back. 'Jase, wait, if you look inside the book later you'll see a time and place on one of the pages where you'll need to be tomorrow, only this one is not for you to stop a would-be killer but to meet someone. Go there just before midnight and don't be afraid of the things you'll see... they're not what they seem.'

Jason had curiosity written all over his face. 'She wanted me to bring you to her so she could meet you in person,' Lori continued. 'I'm so sorry for what I put you through... but she made me... she made me do all of this.'

Jason could find no response. After wiping the tears off Lori's face he kissed her forehead and left the Future Assassin to face her fate alone.

The flashing lights of several police cars and an ambulance lit up the walls of the houses waking the residents who peered from their windows in bewilderment as a couple of uniformed officers escorted Lori to one of the vehicles.

Jason could barely watch as Lori spotted him standing among a group of nosy neighbours who had come out into the cold in their night clothes to get a better view. He felt his heart sink at the sad smile she gave him before she was shoved into the back seat of the squad car which sped off into the night taking her out of his life forever.

*

Jason waited until the coast was clear before going in search of the car which he found parked in a side street not far from where Lori had been arrested.

As soon as he got into the driver's seat he retrieved the mysterious book from the back seat. It was two inches thick and about as large as his hand, its binding worn and faded. Although it looked like any other notebook there was something strange about it that made him feel uncertain about whether to open it or not.

He eventually pulled open the dark leather cover. A musty smell filled his nostrils and he saw Lori's clumsy handwriting covering page after page from top to bottom detailing events from the future with the names of each would-be killer she had successfully assassinated crossed out in red ink. As he turned the pages he came across an old photo she had been using as a bookmark. It was a picture of Lori as a young girl standing outside a chrome gypsy caravan with people he thought were her parents and baby brother. He smiled at the sight of her happy face posing for the camera before putting the photo aside and turning back to the pages to find out where the next events were going to take him.

One or two other names were crossed off as he squinted at the list and at the bottom of the page saw the details of where he needed to be the next day: 'Be at Pembrey Forest, Carmarthenshire, just before midnight on 25/12 to meet the White Lady. Bring a torch to follow the path to the clearing where she resides next to the old oak.'

Jason felt the hairs on the back of his neck stand up as he read the note over and over till he could almost memorise it word for word. Who was this mysterious White Lady that Lori was in league with he wondered, returning the photograph between the pages and closing the book. And what was Lori talking about when she warned him not to be frightened by what he'd see?

He couldn't make any sense of it so with only one thing left to do he started the car and headed for the next destination ready to confront whatever was waiting for him in Pembrey Forest.

CHAPTER 12 - TWISTS OF FATE

It was Christmas morning when Jason arrived in Carmarthenshire. The roads were deserted and although the sky was laden with snow it only fell in brief flurries. Feeling tired after all the hours of driving he'd endured over the past few days, he pulled into a small layby and decided to get an hour or two's sleep before continuing his journey.

When he finally woke it was dark. He switched on the car light to check his watch and realised that he'd overslept by seven or eight hours. The time read 8.15 pm and with only a few hours left to find Pembrey Forest he set off once more, stopping only once at a petrol station to ask for directions.

The grey-haired man on duty patiently gave Jason the information he needed before telling him about the area's notorious history. 'One of the most haunted places in Britain, I should be warning you,' said the man in a strong local accent. 'I wouldn't be going anywhere near there at this time of night if I were you.'

Jason smiled in disbelief as he lingered by the entrance. 'Haunted?'

'You better believe it's haunted, friend. People come from all over to visit the forest, especially at Halloween, and nine times out of ten they come back with stories of apparitions, strange orbs floating above the trees, faces appearing in photos that weren't seen when the picture was taken... there's even those who claim to have encountered UFOs... not to mention all the other tales about the White Lady.' The man shook his head as he returned to the paper he'd been reading.

'White Lady?' said Jason, thinking of what Lori had written in the book.

'Yeah, you know, the one they say haunts the small clearing near the oak tree with the creepy face on its trunk. Blimey, call yourself a tourist, you must know something about the place or you wouldn't be wasting Christmas paying it a visit,' said the man, looking at Jason over the top of his glasses.

'Well, I've heard bits and pieces,' said Jason, opening the door. 'Thanks for filling me in on a few other things though.'

'Yeah, well you be careful now mind… and just make sure you stay on the footpath or you'll never find your way out of there.'

The man went back to his paper not realising that he was talking to himself until he heard the door shut.

Tall trees blotted out the moonlit sky as Jason drove carefully along the winding lane that led to the forest. Drooping branches on both sides of the road scraped against the roof of the car as if the trees were alive and trying to reach out with their twiggy fingers to stop him going any further. Then he was through the trees and the way ahead opened up to the cloudless sky once more.

Ahead Jason could see the lights of some caravans that were parked up on the verge. Curious and unfriendly faces of women and children stared out at him from each decorated window as he slowly drove by, while a small army of dogs left to roam wild chased after the car barking and snapping at the wheels. Further on, near a few parked pick-up trucks and vans, a group of men warmed themselves by a fire, laughing and drinking as the flames crackled and leapt up in front of them. As Jason got closer one of the men left his companions to stop the car in the middle of the road. He was shifty-looking with dark hair and shooed the dogs away before tapping on the window with his gold ring.

Jason opened his window halfway. 'There's nothing up there for you, friend, only a dead end,' said the gypsy in an accent that sounded similar to Lori's.

'I know, I just fancy a stroll through the woods,' replied Jason.

The man took a swig from a can of lager then bent down beside the window. 'So you're looking for a few ghosties are ya?' he grinned flashing a gold tooth. 'Well, you've come to the right place. Rather you than me though, pal, but good luck and a merry Christmas to ya all the same.'

The gypsy straightened up and chuckled as he shook Jason by the hand before staggering back to his friends who watched with curiosity as Jason drove on.

He parked the car where the lane ended at the edge of the woods and was relieved to find a torch in the boot before he attempted to follow the path into the forest. The moonlight made the snow-covered trees glow eerily and a slight breeze swept through their branches as if they were parting to invite him inside.

'Why did it have to be midnight?' Jason grumbled to himself before reluctantly taking his first steps into the unknown. There was nothing to frighten him at first, twigs broke under his feet and fallen branches attempted to trip him up as he ventured deeper into the wood where the light was scarce and the naked limbs of the trees huddled closer together over the icy path.

Startled by a rustling noise from behind him Jason turned and flashed his torch on whatever was approaching but saw only the same terriers that had earlier chased his car excitedly wagging their tails as they ran around his legs. Glad of their company, he whistled for them to follow him as he continued his walk.

He pushed past overhanging branches and stepped over a tangle of weeds and bushes in an attempt not to lose sight of the path through the forest that seemed to go on for ever.

Ominous silhouettes lurked against the skyline accompanied by strange noises that he tried hard to convince himself were just his imagination. Then in one heart-stopping moment he heard a chilling voice calling his name from somewhere close by.

Snow crunched under his feet as he stepped off the path and into the undergrowth following the sound of the voice until the trees began to give way and he found himself standing at the edge of a small clearing.

Jason flashed his torch around the glade. The ancient oak tree, its gnarled trunk resembling a human face, came into view confirming that this was the place where he needed to be. There was no sign of the Lady in White who Lori had said would be waiting to meet him; he could no longer hear the voice that had been calling him and, apart from the rustle of the dogs in the undergrowth, all was quiet.

The torch began to flicker, the surrounding trees groaned and creaked as a gust of wind pierced their branches moving them back and forth as if some unnatural force was sweeping through the forest charging the air with an energy that he found hard to explain.

'Jason…' the same voice called again, grabbing his attention while he flashed his failing torch searching for the source.

Finally, it went out and by the light from the moon he saw a hooded figure standing perfectly still beside the ancient oak.

The terriers who had tagged along with him so bravely for most of the journey began to growl and bark at the motionless figure. Just as terrified by what they saw, Jason turned his head and considered following them as they ran back the way they had come.

'Don't be afraid of the strange things you'll see, they're not what they seem,' Lori's words echoed in his mind forcing him to turn around and face his fears. He looked back to where he'd seen the apparition but it had already disappeared.

Jason headed towards the oak tree that stood in solitary splendour in the middle of the clearing its sagging branches touching the ground resembling the legs of a spider. The earth was damp under his feet as he approached the tree trying in vain to get the torch to work.

As he reached the spot where he'd first seen the ghostly figure a rush of warm air filled his lungs as though he was stepping from the depths of winter and walking into a mid-summer's evening. Before his eyes, a blanket of green leaves spread across the oak's naked branches and at the foot of the ancient tree wild flowers carpeted the ground.

Jason backed up a few steps and felt the temperature plummet, the leaves vanished from the oak's branches and the wild flowers disappeared one by one. He stepped forward again, the warmth returned and the leaves and wild flowers reappeared.

He walked up to the tree and knelt before its branches. A bee flew past his face as he reached out to pick a flower from the tall grass but it slipped through his fingers as if it were a mirage.

Jason heard a noise behind him but before he dared to stand up and confront whatever was approaching he knew that it was the White Lady coming to meet him. He turned and stood in amazement; he wanted to speak but his voice had left him, he wanted to run but his whole body was frozen.

The White Lady stood perfectly still in front him, the hood of her white cloak concealing her eyes and nose, and even though he was accustomed to seeing things that were out of the ordinary during his adventures with Lori over the past few days, nothing could have prepared him for this.

'Wh… what are you?' he stuttered, unable to stop his voice from shaking.

An extended silence followed before the White Lady finally spoke. 'What do you think I am?' she asked in a voice like the sound of the wind.

'I'm not sure…' Jason replied, noticing that her body was transparent. 'Are you a ghost?' he dared to ask.

'No more of a ghost than you are to me,' the White Lady answered with a smile curling the corners of her mouth.

'I don't understand.'

'All shall be revealed to you shortly, Jason, but first you must tell me where the gypsy girl is.'

'She's not here… I came alone. Lori… she's been arrested,' he replied, nervously anticipating the White Lady's reaction.

'Arrested?' said the White Lady, remaining perfectly still despite the surprised tone in her unearthly voice. 'Poor child,' she said gravely. 'But at least we now have you to replace her.'

'You seem to know who I am, so why don't you tell me who you are,' he said with a tremble in his voice that he could not hide.

A haunting smile returned to the White Lady's lips before she spoke. 'Do not be afraid of me, Jason, for I am not a spirit of the deceased or a ghostly apparition... I am as alive and human as you are. The only difference between you and me is that I'm from one era of time and you are from another.'

'That doesn't make sense.'

'Then I shall do my best to explain so that you may understand. Anomalies in nature have been occurring in certain places around the world for aeons. Throughout history there are stories of hauntings and encounters with ghosts, strange flying objects in the sky, or meetings with terrifying monsters in the forests and oceans. But they are simply misunderstood. In reality these sightings and experiences are nothing more than a freak act of nature showing a glimpse of things that either have been or will be as one era entwines with another.' She interlaced her bony fingers, 'Just as it does right here and now for you and me. You see, Jason, this is one of the many known locations on earth where every so often, be it lengthy or brief, times collide. Where I stand for you is the future and where you stand for me is the past.'

'So what's happening here is all down to some sort of time slip?' said Jason beginning to understand.

'Not a slip, a clash, an abnormality where the laws of nature are turned upside down and fantasy meets reality.'

'But how is that possible?'

'No one knows for sure how or why a time clash occurs. Mother Earth has many secrets, some of which will never be properly understood. But there are those of us who believe that these anomalies occur for a reason; to allow humanity to correct mistakes from the past to create a better future.'

'So, you're from the future; how far into the future?' Jason asked.

'The timeline between these collisions can be thousands, even millions, of years apart. The one between yours and mine, however, is much less.'

'Yet still far enough for you to tell Lori the names of all the would-be killers from our time period so she could write them down and you could have her assassinate them.' Jason sounded angry.

The White Lady hung her head despondently. 'Poor child... she was just a little girl when she first saw me. Her family had settled down the lane during their summer travels, and a game of truth or dare with her friends led her here to me. She was scared when I approached her; she ran away believing that I was a ghost, and I didn't see her again until she returned years later as a young woman. Only this time she wasn't scared; her parents and her younger brother had been killed in a racist attack and she came in search of me seeking comfort in knowing that if there were such things as ghosts then there would also be such a thing as an afterlife where she would see her loved ones again.

'After revealing to her what I've just told you, I realised the only comfort I could offer was to give her the names of all the would-be killers in her country from her time period so that at least no one else would have to suffer the same horrors as she. But the task was too much for her to take on alone. She asked me to find her help so I brought her to you... and now you must take over from where she left off... you must replace her as the Future Assassin.'

'No! I will stop these terrible things from happening but I won't kill anyone. Things are going to be done differently now, the way they should always have been.'

The White Lady lifted her head. 'You can't do that,' she said, a storm brewing in her unearthly voice.

'I can, and I will, and there's nothing you can do about it. You won't twist me like you did Lori,' replied Jason with confidence. 'I have the book in my possession and everything I need to know is in those pages... so I have nothing more to say to you, except that this is the last time we shall see each other.'

'I knew it was a mistake getting her to save you,' she said, stopping Jason in his tracks as he prepared to leave. A confused expression clouded his face as he turned to see the White Lady standing perfectly still, her back turned to him.

'What are you talking about? No one saved me.'

'Yes she did, Jason, the gypsy girl saved you from being killed by Harry on the night of the party.'

'Harry? Harry killed himself and took my family with him,' Jason reminded her.

'No, Jason, Harry cared for your family, he would never hurt them; it was you he wanted dead, not them and not himself… he left in a hurry that night because he had learnt the truth about you and Jessica. To prevent you and her from being together he hatched a plan to sneak into your house that night and kill you while you were drunk.'

She slowly turned to face him. 'You see, when the gypsy girl asked me to find her a partner I immediately thought of you because of your professional skills, but I knew you wouldn't be persuaded so easily. I knew that your spirit would have to be broken first, so to convince you to join us I had to make you believe that Harry killed himself and your family in a deliberate car crash… when the truth is Harry didn't kill them at all… the gypsy girl did!'

'No… it can't be true,' said Jason, not wanting to believe what he was hearing.

The White Lady gave a rueful smile. 'Oh, she didn't want to do it, believe me she didn't… she begged me to find another way, but I convinced her. I told her that it was for the greater good and in the end she reluctantly agreed, and on the night of the party she loosened the wheel bolts on Harry's car sealing all your fates with one simple move.'

'No! You're lying,' said Jason, backing away from her as Lori's words echoed in his mind: 'I'm so sorry for what I've put you through… but she made me… she made me do all of this.'

'So you see, Jason, I'm the one pulling the strings, just as I always have been. You think you can defy me, but I will find a way to stop you… I will find a way to have the gypsy girl released.' She advanced towards him and spoke in a thunderous voice: 'You will never win, Jason, do you hear me? You will never win.'

She laughed as he screamed in anguish and chucked his broken torch at her in rage. But it passed straight through her body and landed on the ground. Her wicked laugh echoed round the glade and she threw back her hood revealing an ancient face etched with wrinkles and silver hair that hung loose around her bony shoulders.

Jason plunged blindly into the darkness of the trees wanting to put as much distance as possible between himself and the White Lady whose laughter still echoed around him. Without a light to guide him he was soon lost in a never-ending maze of terror where the ghostly faces of children peered at him from behind the trees and half-bodied apparitions met him at every turn.

He desperately tried to find the way out until his progress was halted by a fallen branch and he tripped and fell, hitting his head hard on a log. As he lay winded on the ground semi-conscious he became aware of dozens of glowing orbs appearing from nowhere illuminating the darkness like nothing he had ever seen before.

Jason watched in wonder as the strange yellow lights gathered around him like moths to a flame and he lost consciousness altogether.

EPILOGUE

Crusty patches of snow crunched beneath Rachel's boots. She stopped and gazed up at the fireworks welcoming in the New Year. A slight breeze picked up a page from last week's paper at her feet with Lori pictured on the front beneath the headline 'Face of The Assassin'. She grabbed at it as it floated past her, disposed of it in the overstuffed bin from where it had come, and continued the rest of her journey home along the deserted streets. It had been an exhausting eight-hour shift.

She heard footsteps close behind her accompanied by the sound of heavy breathing and before she could turn to see who it was someone grabbed her by the arm.

'Gary... you scared me half to death, don't sneak up on me like that,' she said, partly annoyed and partly relieved to see her husband.

'Sorry, I didn't mean to scare you,' he said, laughing apologetically.

'What are you doing here anyway? I thought you were going over to a friend's house for a few drinks.' Rachel was still a little shaken.

'I was, but then I decided that I'd rather walk my lovely wife home instead.'

'I think I'm old enough to walk myself home, thank you,' she said, taking off her officer's hat to finger comb her hair.

They carried on walking without speaking for a moment or so until Gary broke the silence. 'I've noticed you've been a little strange lately. It's Jason, isn't it? You're worried about him.'

They stopped and Rachel nodded. 'It's been a week now and I haven't heard a word from him.'

'Look, I'm sure wherever he is he's doing fine,' said Gary reassuringly. 'If he wasn't you'd more than likely have heard something by now.'

'I know, but I'm just a bit concerned because the last time I saw him he was talking like I was never going to see him again. Gary, what if he's done something stupid... what if he was trying to tell me something that night and I misunderstood him?'

'Shhh... Don't think such things or there'll be no end to it,' Gary interrupted. 'Rachel, you've been a good friend to him and you've done all you can to help, but you can't watch over him for ever; it's down to him now, he has his own path to follow and wherever it's going to lead I'm sure it'll bring him home eventually. Now, try to stop worrying... everything will be fine, I promise.'

She seemed comforted by his words and smiled as he playfully put her officer's hat on his own head and threw an arm around her shoulders. 'Come on, Mrs Summers, let's get you home.'

They carried on walking and talking until they reached a dimly lit underpass. Two thuggish-looking skinheads lurked at the far end moving towards them. Gary removed Rachel's hat and held her more tightly while slowing his pace. Rachel knew there and then that he had the same feeling of dread about the men as she did.

'Are you Rachel Summers?' asked one of the men, standing with folded arms blocking them from passing.

She looked nervously at her husband before answering, 'Yes… but…'

'We've been waiting for you,' said the other man, cutting her off.

She was about to reply when she heard footsteps coming up behind her. 'Hello, friends' said a rasping voice.

Rachel turned to see another skinhead approaching. 'Sorry to spoil your evening, but we've been sent on a little errand for someone by the name of Rick Daxton.'

'Daxton?' she queried in a panicky voice.

'Name rings a bell does it, luv?' The man laughed before he continued, 'You see, as you've probably heard he 'as an appeal coming up soon and the word on the street is that the man who 'ad him put away for trying to rob a post office 'as done a disappearing act, leaving only one other witness who could ruin his chances of an early release… who, I'm afraid to say, is you! Now, usually in cases like this we would've asked you to change your statement… but, unfortunately, Mr Daxton doesn't believe you'll be persuaded so easily, which leaves us with only one alternative...'

The man signalled for his two companions to pull Gary away while he grabbed Rachel and pinned her against the graffiti-covered wall. Gary desperately tried to free himself so that he could get back to his wife, but a blow to the head knocked him out and the thugs let him fall to the ground.

'You get over there and make sure no one is coming from that end and you do the same at the other'. The man dished out orders, then pulled out a wicked-looking knife and held it against Rachel's throat.

'Please,' she begged, 'you don't have to do this... I have two children...'

'Shut up,' the man spat. 'You should've thought of that before you started poking your nose where it don't belong.'

Tears streamed down Rachel's cheeks and she closed her eyes, bracing herself for what might happen next. The lights of the underpass flickered eerily and one of the thugs cried out in pain as he was struck hard on the head.

The remaining two looked in the direction of the sound and to their dismay saw a hooded figure standing over their friend's unconscious body before he turned and headed in their direction.

The thug guarding the opposite end of the underpass grabbed a taser gun from inside his jacket and ran to meet the hooded figure in the middle of the tunnel. It took only moments for him to be disarmed and left lying on the ground having been hit over the head with his own weapon.

'Don't come any closer,' said the leader, who was using Rachel to shield him as he slowly backed down the tunnel still holding his knife to her throat. The lights flickered again and died. In the darkness the stranger managed to grab the thug's knife, release Rachel and drop the leader with a shot from the taser as he made a run for the entrance.

Rachel seemed frozen in shock. 'Are you ok?' he asked in a voice that sounded all too familiar.

She nodded as he handed her something, which she could just about see in the orange glow of a nearby street lamp – it was a small memory stick. 'The police are on their way,' he said. 'When they get here give that to them; it's a video recording showing what these three were planning to do.'

'I will, I promise,' she said, hearing the police sirens in the distance. 'Thank you for saving my life.'

'Thank you for saving mine.' He smiled as he slipped something else into her hand, then turned and walked away out of the underpass.

The lights flickered back on allowing Rachel to run to her husband and help him up. 'Gary, are you ok?'

'I'm fine,' he said, slowly coming back to his senses. 'How about you, are you alright?'

She wiped her eyes and nodded. 'What happened?' Gary asked, shocked to see the three attackers sprawled on the ground.

'Someone helped us.'

'Helped us?' Gary looked confused as Rachel walked back to the tunnel entrance and watched the hooded figure slowly walk away into the distance beneath the fireworks that lit up the night sky.

He moved to join her. 'Rachel, who helped us?'

She removed the gold pendant from the small pouch in her hand and smiled, knowing that the mysterious man who had saved their lives was Jason.

It was a New Year and new beginnings – perhaps he had found his true vocation at last.

Published by

www.publishandprint.co.uk

THANKS FOR
READING, PLEASE
GIVE AN HONEST
REVIEW ON
AMAZON.

ED JONES